## He leaned over and silenced her with a kiss as he pulled her tight against him.

She could feel his arousal pushing against her and all she wanted was to give every ounce of passion she had to him. But this wasn't the place, not here on a plane with their client only yards away from them. It couldn't happen and she wanted so badly for it to happen.

Her heart pounded and something deep inside wanted only to melt into him. Her mind screamed to pull away. It couldn't be—this was the wrong time, the wrong place, the wrong man. And yet, her body felt differently.

She put her hands on his shoulder, creating a suggestion of distance between them.

"Jade."

"No." She shook her head. For as much as she wanted him against her, as much as she wanted his lips ravishing hers, as much as she wanted all of it and more, she couldn't.

She was a professional agent and she refused to sleep with her boss. No matter how good she knew it would be.

# SHEIK'S RESCUE

---

## RYSHIA KENNIE

HARLEQUIN INTRIGUE®

Every girl should be as lucky as me to have a spare mother.
Ma D—for all the moments you listened and all the thoughtful
advice you gave. Raise your teacup. This one is for you.

ISBN-13: 978-1-335-72100-6

Sheik's Rescue

Recycling programs
for this product may
not exist in your area.

Copyright © 2017 by Patricia Detta

Printed in U.S.A.

www.Harlequin.com

**Ryshia Kennie** has received a writing award from the City of Regina, Saskatchewan, and was also a semifinalist for the Kindle Book Awards. She finds that there's never a lack of places to set an edge-of-the-seat suspense, as prairie winters find her dreaming of warmer places for heart-stopping stories. They are places where deadly villains threaten intrepid heroes and heroines who battle for their right to live or even to love. For more, visit ryshiakennie.com.

## Books by Ryshia Kennie

### Harlequin Intrigue

#### *Desert Justice*

*Sheik's Rule*
*Sheik's Rescue*

*Suspect Witness*

# CAST OF CHARACTERS

*Sheik Zafir Al-Nassar*—Second eldest of the Al-Nassar brothers, he provides backup to both the Moroccan and Wyoming office of Nassar Security. He plays the field. But when he partners with Jade on a case that takes a turn that threatens her life, he finds that falling in love is second only to saving her life.

*Jade Van Everett*—Loves everything about her job, especially the risk. But with Zafir risk has gone to a new level. She's falling in love and can't stop it. And in Morocco, without Zafir, it is possible that she might not make it home alive.

*Sheik Faisal Al-Nassar*—The head of the Wyoming branch of Nassar Security.

*Sheik Emir Al-Nassar*—The eldest of the Al-Nassar brothers, he runs the Moroccan branch of Nassar Security.

*Sheik Talib Al-Nassar*—Zafir's younger brother. He's based out of Marrakesh.

*Prince Sadiq el Eloua*—Known as Stanley. Is he as socially inept as he appears or is there something more behind his alleged photography trip to Wyoming?

*Prince Rashad*—A Moroccan royal responsible for Stanley's lax security detail.

*Chasi el Eloua*—Stanley's older brother died in a psychiatric hospital years ago, or did he?

*Khaled el Eloua*—Stanley's elderly uncle. With a fortune up for grabs no one is safe.

*Fayad el Eloua*—a nephew of Khaled el Eloua. Would he take Stanley out for an inheritance?

*Mohammed Jadid*—Stanley's cousin is unrelated to Khaled el Eloua but he has followed Stanley to Wyoming. He may die with his secrets.

# Chapter One

The howl of a lone wolf cut through the gray Wyoming sky, shattering the valley's early-morning silence. The howl echoed across the sharp lines of the Teton mountain range, which rose in a jagged line against the horizon. The raw cry broke through the unseasonably late April snow as it drifted down in a freezing veil that covered the prairie grass surrounding Nassar Security.

On his office balcony just outside Jackson, Wyoming, Vice President Zafir Al-Nassar took a deep breath. A sense of foreboding ran through him. Normally he would have enjoyed the reflective stillness of the late-spring snowfall, but now his thoughts were elsewhere. He wasn't sure what he was looking for. There was nothing disturbing the area except the blanket of snow that covered everything. It seemed to mock his unease as it powdered the nearby landscape and the roofs of the distant houses. It was Hollywood snow, big white flakes coming down in a gentle curtain beneath a still sky. It was the kind of weather that the film industry sometimes chased through the northern states and Canada. His thoughts were broken as, in the distance, he saw a dirt bike buzzing along the road that ran along the interstate.

He rubbed his temple. He'd had a low-grade headache all morning. He'd been up too late last night trying out the limits of an online game his brother Faisal had shown him a few days earlier. They'd played it a number of times while he'd been in Marrakech and Faisal had been here in Wyoming. He'd been looking forward to playing it with him in person when he arrived in Wyoming. He'd been disappointed to find Faisal was on assignment on the East Coast, departing just before his arrival. He'd just arrived with his sister, Tara, from Marrakech, Morocco, via New York, only thirty-five hours ago. Yesterday afternoon he'd seen her off on the last leg of her return journey to the university via the company jet. The travel, the online game, all of it combined into too many days with too little sleep. He stuffed his hand into the pocket of his low-rise jeans.

"Idiot," he muttered as he watched the motorcycle. Driving a bike in this kind of weather was, across the board, a bad idea. He shook his head and would have lost interest, except for the fact that minutes later, the bike turned into his parking lot.

"What the…" His mouth was set in a grim line. Could this be one of the employees from the Wyoming branch of Nassar? Who else would come out here on a Saturday? They didn't hire risk-adverse individuals, but they didn't hire thrill-seekers, either. Both personality types came with their own set of problems. He stayed where he was, intrigued by whom it might be as the bike swerved in a wide arc and pulled in beside his rental. Minutes passed. The rider seemed to be fiddling with something on the bike. It was an older model dirt bike—even worse as far as handling on slick roads. The driver might be a teenager.

He shook his head. That was an ageist thought, but he couldn't imagine who else would be crazy enough to chance riding such a vehicle in this weather. With the driver's back to him it was hard to tell. What he could tell was that he wasn't very big; at least, he had no bulk to him. It looked like he was tall but other than...

The man pulled off the helmet. Black hair fell to his shoulders. He turned around. The gray bomber jacket was half zipped, and it was now clear that this was no man. She held a helmet by its straps as she threaded her fingers through her hair and stopped as her eyes locked with his.

Jade Van Everett. The face and the picture on the file snapped together in his mind like an errant jigsaw puzzle. She was the agent assigned to their latest case. He wasn't familiar with her, at least not in person. She'd been with the agency only a little over a year, and both times he'd been here, she'd been either on a case or on vacation. But he was very familiar with who she was on paper. Twenty-nine to his thirty-one, her track record was impressive and the fact that she was easy on the eye, a bonus. Again, all of it had only been on paper. Yet he knew in his gut that Jade was different.

Jade... He felt that he knew her so much deeper than he should. She'd fascinated him before he'd ever physically laid eyes on her. But it was her accomplishments in the field that really impressed him, not her picture in the file. He'd studied every angle of the cases she'd been assigned with Nassar and was familiar with her past record with the agency. He knew her like he knew no other agent, and he refused to let himself consider why that might be.

The case she was assigned to now was the same one that had found him at the office this early in the morning. He'd been making sure that everything, as low-key as it was, went off without a hitch. As a family operation, Nassar Security depended on him to manage either the Morocco or Wyoming office at a moment's notice.

This case involved a Moroccan prince. In fact, it had been Moroccan royalty who had hired the company to provide security for the minor royal, who was visiting Wyoming. The client was a cousin too many times removed from the current king of Morocco to ever attain power, and he wasn't wealthy.

That eliminated two factors that might threaten his safety. Except for the weak link to royalty, there was nothing special about the man. Thus, only one agent, Jade Van Everett, had been assigned.

In the file picture her hair had been lighter, shorter—her expression more serious. She was an extraordinarily good-looking woman even on file, but the paper copy didn't reflect the vibrant beauty that the real woman possessed. It was hard not to stare, for he was caught by surprise.

Now that she'd finished with the bike, she wasted no time in striding across the small lot, her attention focused on him with a look that hinted at trouble. This was clearly a woman with an issue, and as he was the only person here, he could only assume that the issue was with him.

So much for quietly sliding into the pulse of the business, he thought.

She had trouble branded on the tight line of her full red lips and in the frown that cut between her delicate, well-defined dark brows.

While he felt the chill in her azure eyes slice through him as she came closer, he couldn't help but admire her figure. He pulled his gaze up from her full bust and met her slightly sarcastic look as she stood on the bottom step looking up.

"Have you seen enough?" she drawled. Her voice was surprisingly relaxed despite the flashing accusation in her look.

She had spunk to go along with her success.

"Maybe," he replied easily, while at the same time he was fully aware that he deserved every ounce of her sarcasm. The accusation in her eyes faded, and he could tell from the softening of her lips that she'd decided to not push the issue. He admired her for that.

"I'm Zafir," he began, taking a step forward.

"I know," she said in her husky voice, and came up a few more steps. "You're why I'm here. I wanted to meet you in person before I picked up the client."

Her eyes raked over him as if she, too, had studied him through his work. He imagined that if she was as good as her file suggested, then that was the case. One didn't come in blind to anything, not a Nassar agent. They were all good, but to be in the top few meant that you left nothing to chance.

Professional, he thought, despite the bike. She smiled and threaded her fingers through her hair, pushing the shining black curtain up and away from her face. She came up another step. They were only a few feet apart.

She put one hand on the railing and held out the other to him. He took it and was caught in a firm grip that held no hesitation.

"What I'd like to know is why Prince Sadiq el Eloua is flying here alone on a commercial airline," she said as she let go of his hand. She was referring to the client. The one she was assigned to. "I know it's too late to do anything about it but really, even if there's no identified threat, at the least he should have been accompanied."

"There's apparently never been a security issue—he has no money or status," he said, realizing that she'd mirrored many of his first doubts. "It appears more for ego that we were hired."

"Seems like there should be more to this, otherwise there's no need to hire us."

He shrugged. "Overkill on Prince Rashad's part," he said, referring to the crown prince next in line to rule Morocco. "An easy assignment for you."

There was something in her eyes and the way she looked at him that, if he were a vain man, he would have called admiration. Instead, it struck him how much the agency had grown, and how often, despite being vice president, he was faced with this situation—where he didn't know the people in his employ. Not that he was complaining; his youngest brother Faisal ran this branch and had done so more than competently.

Jade brushed past him and headed toward the entrance to his office. She pulled the door open and walked in as if it were hers. "While I'm here I want to check the file one last time before I pick him up," she said over her shoulder.

He followed her inside, closing the door behind him as a drift of snow skimmed the heated cork floor and immediately began to melt. He walked over to where she stood by his desk.

"You've had it out?" she asked as she picked up the only file on his desk. She did so without hesitation. But that was how Faisal's office ran, with casual efficiency. While the Marrakech office had gone completely digital, Faisal still insisted on paper files. He loved all things retro. Retro had never appealed to Zafir. He'd take the latest smartphone over the century-old wooden file cabinet that stood in a corner of the office.

He watched her review the file. He assumed that she was going over details that she'd seen before. They were details that he'd just familiarized himself with. His mind reviewed what he knew of the client. The man was an amateur photographer. He was months short of his fortieth birthday and attached to nothing, not family, career, not even a stable home. He was rather like a man a decade or two younger. The majority of his income came from a life insurance policy that he'd received after the death of his parents. He supplemented that by occasionally selling his photos to magazines. That was why he was here, to take outdoor pictures of the Jackson Hole valley. It was the one thing he had in common with the client: they both felt the allure of Wyoming's wild beauty. The file lay open where Jade had dropped it. He looked down and a chubby-cheeked man smiled back at him.

"Twenty-fifth in line to the throne," Jade's voice

interrupted his private assessment. "My instinct says that's important."

Instinct, he couldn't dispute that. It was what separated the good agent from the excellent.

She went to the window and stood there as snow hit, melted and slid down the glass. He took the file from the desk, closed it and put it back into the cabinet.

"He arrives in under two hours." She glanced at her watch as she turned around. "I just can't get over it. I mean, he's a royal, I'm to make sure he's safe, and yet he's flying halfway across the world alone." She shrugged. "That's why his lineage was grating on me. But even twenty-fifth, with zero chance of ever attaining the throne... There's safety in numbers, in having someone trained to watch out for you. Someone who pays attention to the surroundings to..." She trailed off. But he could see her frustration. Her blue eyes were alight with passion and concern.

"I'm not sure how it went down. He shouldn't be flying either alone or commercial. What I know is that Prince Rashad isn't happy about it. I wouldn't be surprised if it's our client's doing." He shrugged. "Anyway, he isn't our problem. At least, not until he lands..."

She frowned. "Despite what I just said, it's a low-key case. Let's just hope he gets here safely." She paused, her attention not on him but on a point somewhere outside the office.

"There's nothing we can do about it."

"You're right," she said. "Our job begins as soon as they have wheels on the ground." She looked at her watch. "I should get moving."

"What's with the dirt bike?" He couldn't help but ask.

She shrugged and looked slightly sheepish. "My pickup wouldn't start this morning. I'm going to get a rental on the way to the airport."

"I'll give you a lift."

"No." She shook her head. "The rental agency is only a few miles up the road. Besides, I love riding the bike in fresh snow," she said. "I'd take it to the airport but I doubt Prince Sadiq would like riding on the back."

From what he'd seen of Jade, he doubted that Prince Sadiq would mind at all.

"I'm not looking forward to it." She paused. "Didn't you find it strange—the name he prefers?" It was the name that neither of them had yet used.

"A bit old-fashioned." He slid a hand into his pocket and rubbed an American penny he always carried between his thumb and forefinger. A long time ago his father had given it to him for luck. His father had been a very logical man, but he believed in talismans and luck. His parents had died tragically three days after his father had so casually tossed him the coin. Now he withdrew his hand, curious at her take.

"Stanley?" Her frown deepened. "What Moroccan royal is named Stanley? I mean even as a nickname." Her eyes crinkled as if she were holding back a laugh. "He uses the name exclusively."

"Royalty. Good chance he has an attitude, which will be a challenge," he said, knowing that he should try to be helpful instead of goading her when they both knew that she was stuck with a dull case.

"I'm betting you're right." She pulled a quarter from her pocket. "Want to flip for odds? Heads he's a challenge."

"Tails, I lose," he finished.

She flipped the coin and looked up with a smile. "Heads. Doesn't change the fact that I've got myself a code white."

He smiled at both the tone of her voice and her lighthearted approach that led them to betting on a case. That was a first, but he didn't doubt that Jade was full of surprises—crazy little firsts.

"Code white." She shook her head, her brow furrowed as if the thought of it pained her.

He empathized with her pain. The agency had codes for assignments. They ranged from the least dangerous, white, to the most, red. There wasn't an agent at Nassar who didn't dread a code white. They were well-paid assignments that were the bread and butter of the agency. But they were also, as in this case, ten days of guaranteed boredom.

She waved as she turned to leave.

"Take a good book," he called after her.

She gave him a look that would have torched a lesser man.

He only laughed.

Jade van Everett had been a pleasant surprise.

*Three days earlier*

THE SMALL STONE house had stood on the edge of the massive estate outside Rabat, Morocco, for generations. It had survived two world wars. Now, an explosion rattled the windows of the main house and blew the roof off the small stone house. The outer walls held for seconds after the initial explosion before the shock rippled through the structure and caused the small building to fall inward. The resulting fire licked quickly through the old wood and paper within the building. The smoke curled easily into the still air. It wasn't until the building was engulfed in flames and the last wall had collapsed that sirens could be heard. By then, it was too late. It was exactly as he had planned. Time would take care of the rest.

His jaw tensed as he looked around in the dim light of the plane's cabin. A young woman stood up two rows ahead of him and stretched. Behind him someone coughed. He covered his mouth and nose with the back of his hand. He hated flying, hated the people, the tight space, the snotty flight attendants. He hated all of it. He pushed his seat into an upright position and tried to stretch, but one foot was trapped by the seat in front of him. He was stuffed and cramped like he, too, was one of them, like the other nothings on this plane. But he was nothing like any of them—he didn't belong here, and soon they would know it.

He'd like to hurt someone right now. He knew that would make him feel better, but he couldn't do that for obvious reasons. Instead, he relaxed his features and tried to keep a pleasant look on his face. The last thing he needed was to act suspicious so that when they landed he was pulled aside by security. That would have his entry into the States delayed or worse, denied.

*Calm down*, he told himself. There was no reason for any of that to happen. But it wasn't over. His fingernails dug into the armrest. He looked down and forced himself to relax. He'd learned years ago as a child that one must relax to gain control. A strap against bare skin was easier to take if one was relaxed rather than tense. It was a tough but useful life skill. He looked furtively around him. But there was nothing unusual. The lights dimmed, and ahead of him a reading light clicked on. To his left was an empty seat and beside that was an elderly woman who'd been snoring off and on since takeoff.

He closed his eyes even as he knew that he couldn't sleep. Minutes passed. He opened his eyes, and his thoughts went back to where they had never left, to all that had transpired. The explosion that was the first step in completing the job he'd been hired for. It was unfortunate that he'd only seen his handi-work from afar, that he couldn't have stayed to hear the man's dying screams. Instead, he'd had to leave, catching the explosion from a distance, seeing the lick of flames and knowing he was one death away from the cash prize.

Across the aisle, a middle-aged man snored, lurched forward and shook himself awake.

He looked away. To any of the other passengers he was unmemorable. A swarthy man with a tired expression in the aisle seat of the Boeing 737. He feigned reading a newspaper. His left ankle was crossed over his right. He ran a hand along the seam of his pant leg. He scowled and then glanced at the watch on his right wrist. He moved the silver band back and forth as if that would adjust the time, but no matter how he looked at it, there were still hours before they landed.

He shoved the paper into the flap in the seat in front of him and looked up. He smiled at the pass-ing flight attendant and thought how he'd like to twist her slim neck until it snapped. He forced his eyes closed, and smiled for the first time since he'd gotten the news. For it was in Jackson, Wyoming, where he'd finally finish what had begun so long ago.

## Chapter Two

*Take a good book.*

It was a lighthearted statement. At least that's what she had thought at the time. Now Zafir's comment held new meaning. At the airport, the client's round, olive-toned face had lit up at the sight of her as if she were a prize in a game of chance. But an hour later, she would have preferred the company of a good book to the client's chatter and fawning eyes.

She remembered trying to lead him through the airport. He'd been distracted by everything. He'd stopped to stare out a window, claiming that he hadn't seen anything so beautiful as that particular view of the Teton Mountains. And when she finally got his attention again, he'd asked that she call him Stanley and then followed her to collect his luggage. She'd had to nudge the duffel under his arm as she gathered his bags. She'd updated him on his living arrangements as she ushered him to the rental vehicle, but she wasn't sure if he heard a word of it.

At the van, she'd slid the door shut after wrestling his bags into the backseat. Stanley had dropped the duffel by the back door and taken his seat without asking whether she needed help with his luggage.

On the way into Jackson, she asked him about the obviously expensive Nikon camera that he pulled out of its case shortly after they left the terminal. That's when she'd found out that Stanley was a talker, at least about his passion—photography.

"How much farther?" His voice would have been average except for the slightly nasal whine.

"Five minutes," she said shortly. She could feel his gaze on her but kept her attention on the snowy, and now icy, road. Her knuckles were white, and it wasn't because of the driving conditions. She knew admiration when she saw it, but she knew it could also turn into something worse. Stanley kept glancing at her in a way she didn't like. She wasn't sure how she was going to make it through an assignment that would be not only a bore but annoying, as well.

"We're here," she said minutes later as she parked the van. It was the only vehicle the rental agency had left that served her purpose. She would upgrade it tomorrow. Once that was done, she could take Stanley to the places he'd identified were perfect for a photo shoot.

"I'd like to take your picture, too, if…"

"No," she bit out. "I'm sorry. That was rather abrupt but no, I'm here to facilitate your trip." An interesting way to put it, she thought. "Not be a subject for your photography," she finished. "I'm sure we'll find more than you can imagine as far as scenery and wildlife to photograph. You don't need me."

"You're beautiful and…"

"No," she repeated. "Enough. This is business, nothing more."

"I'm sorry," he said, looking rather abashed and completely out of his element.

But this time she was sorry, sorry for so many different reasons than he might think. Sorry for making him uncomfortable, sorry for taking this assignment. Although she had to admit that there was no choice in the latter. It hadn't been voluntary.

Her attention went to the building in front of her. This was her headquarters for the duration of Stanley's stay. The three-story red cedar apartment building was small but perfectly situated. She didn't expect anything less. Leslie, Nassar's relocation expert, had scouted the city and located this building. It had all the amenities the client requested as well as being easy to secure. The street was quiet, part residential and part business. Even now, mid-morning on a Saturday, there was little noise other than the soft drone of traffic on nearby roads. Stanley's apartment was located on the second floor. The apartment above was vacant, as was the one below it. Combined with its small size, its low occupancy made the building even more perfect. She'd been briefed on the other occupants. All ten were trouble-free; none of them had criminal records. They ranged from two senior citizens to a professor currently on sabbatical overseas. The ground-floor apartment was assigned to Jade. The location was perfect for her to stay close for the duration of the client's visit.

"Let's go," she said as she unbuckled her seat belt and opened the van door.

No response.

She looked over at Stanley. He wasn't looking at her but rather chewing his lower lip, almost like he hadn't heard her. Maybe he needed a moment, she thought. But her other thought was that the man was a bit odd.

She thought of Zafir. It was hard not to make the comparison between the two men. She had just recently met them both, and they were so completely different. Sinfully good-looking, cocky Zafir, she thought. She shouldn't be thinking of him like that. But it was like she knew him. She'd studied every case he'd worked and heard stories of his exploits from his brother Faisal. In person, Zafir was more gorgeous and sure of himself than a man outside the pages of a men's magazine should be, and yet there was something down to earth about him, too. He'd put her off balance, off her game. As a result, her first reaction was to snap at him.

Stop it, she told herself. He was her boss on this case and not a man to be lusted after. Besides, looks weren't everything. She'd learned that the hard way. Give her a homely man with a great personality any day, or better yet, no man. At least not at the moment. She was enjoying her job too much, current assignment aside.

"This is it," she said to Stanley, who hadn't moved.

He had a slight smile on his face and a glow in his eyes as if excited by the idea, yet he hesitated to open his door.

"What's wrong?"

"Nothing, I…"

He was looking uncertain, as if he had made a bad choice. Fine time to think of that now, she thought, now that he was here. Despite the thought, she was concerned. As long he was in the States he was her problem, and the last thing she needed was for him to fall apart.

His hands shook slightly as he fumbled with the seat belt. "Nothing at all."

"You're sure?"

"Yes. I always react like this after a flight. Kind of a delayed reaction."

An outright lie, she thought, noticing how his voice sounded thinner and he wouldn't look at her. With any luck it was a temporary case of fear of the unknown. "Let's get you settled," she said. She got out and slid open the back door to get his luggage.

"The photography will be amazing," Stanley said from just behind her. Now his voice sounded normal, as if the last few minutes hadn't happened. There was nothing but anticipation in his tone. It was like he was trying too hard to hide his unease. "I can't wait."

"Wyoming is known for that, scenery. A photographer's dream," she agreed as she tried not to let her prejudice for all things Wyoming show. She supposed she'd already failed at that mission with her last sentence.

She went to step back and was stopped by Stanley. "Give me a bit of room," she said as she leaned in and pulled his too-heavy suitcase from the backseat. Too heavy for anyone visiting for only ten days.

"Stanley," she bit out as she backed up and her elbow bumped his soft midsection. "Move."

A few minutes later, she slipped the key in the lock to the apartment door. She could almost feel him breathing. She swung around.

"Look, Stanley." She hesitated, almost stumbling on the name. "If you want me to do my job properly, I need some space." She wondered how many times she'd have to repeat that phrase.

He took a step back. He looked puzzled and anxious. It was becoming like a dance with two mismatched partners. She took a deep breath. As soon as she got his luggage inside, it was a dance that was going to end.

"In fact, wait here. Hold this." She slipped the handle of the suitcase into his hand and turned to push the apartment door open. She was only mildly amused to hear the suitcase thump onto the floor.

"Having trouble?" she asked. She glanced over her shoulder. He was fumbling with his vintage suitcase. It had no wheels and a worn faux-leather cover. It was an oddity. Like Stanley, she thought.

Her hand dropped to her Colt. She had just purchased it. The gun had replaced her old standby Glock that had seen her through her training and first year. The Colt was an exciting purchase. She could hardly wait to see action with this in her hand. But so far, other than target practice, she had yet to use it.

She moved past the entrance, noting everything. White laminate floors, gray walls, a couch to the left, table to the right. There was nothing else. She had to be sure. Stanley and his suitcase were forgotten. This was business. There was nothing but silence and the ticking of... She pulled the Colt, reveling in the feel of it in her hand. Other women loved new clothes. She loved guns. The thought made her smile. Something clicked. She swung, pointing the Colt in the direction of the sound. It was nothing but a wall clock in the kitchen. Someone had plugged it in since the last time she'd been here.

"Is this necessary?" Stanley's frightened voice came from the hallway.

She held up a hand to him, motioning him to be quiet. On another assignment, in a different place, ticking had meant something so much more sinister. This wasn't such a case, she reminded herself. Still, she needed to make sure. No matter the high probability that there was no threat. If there was, she needed to eliminate it. After all, someone had paid her to do just that.

The kitchen and living area gleamed as if they'd been recently cleaned and infrequently used. She took a step in and then two—she did a visual sweep of the area. It was overkill, she knew that, but one could never be too safe. She'd learned that through her arduous FBI training. The experience had been put into practice during the last year with Nassar.

A minute, two—she went through the small one-bedroom apartment. All clear, exactly as it should be. She went to the hallway and gave Stanley what she hoped would be interpreted as a friendly smile. One more come-hither look from him and she might punch him, she thought, knowing that of course she wouldn't. She was too professional for that, but…the thought was out there.

"Let me take that," she said. She lifted his duffel bag and set it on the coffee table. "You might want to take the suitcase into the bedroom."

"Fine," he said, looking slightly bewildered.

She opened the blinds that masked the balcony, letting in a stream of feeble sunlight. The snowstorm was on its last legs. The snowfall was a thin curtain, unlike the thick flakes that had blanketed the area in a layer of white earlier in the day.

"You'll have a good view, and I'll be just down-stairs while you're here."

"Living?" he asked in a puzzled voice.

"Yes. As long as you're here, I will be, too." Exactly ten days, she wanted to say, no more.

His face lit up at that like she'd told him she'd be his best friend. And she supposed that in a way, for a time, she would be.

"There's a beautiful view of the mountains," she said as she slid the glass patio door open. She could smell his aftershave as he approached. She'd first become aware of the scent at the airport terminal, where it had preceded him as he'd disembarked in a cloud that was as pleasant as the lingering smell of cooked fish. She'd felt some sympathy for his seat-mates on the flight and even those who might have been sitting nearby. Stanley wasn't one to slide into the background; everything about him was distinctive.

She turned her attention to the street. A vacant lot was directly across from them. Beside it there was a parking lot with only a few snow-shrouded cars. The lot was blanketed in snow and shadowed by the stark branches of winter-dead trees. She frowned. The trees and shrubs blocked her view. She could see nothing between the parking lot and the low-rise brick building beside it.

"This place is small," Stanley said as he came up too close beside her.

She moved one step over and thought again how this game was getting very old. She glanced at him, but he was looking not at the view but behind her, at the apartment. She turned back to the street.

"That's because it's temporary."

And because they were staying away from the luxury homes and condos that would be harder to secure. She pressed a finger to her temple. She could feel the beginnings of a headache.

He wasn't going away. She needed to deal. She turned to face the only headache she had—Stanley.

"Often the hunters and skiers use this same lodging, but there aren't many around this time of year. Right now there are a few permanents, or longer stays, I guess you'd call them, and you. But you won't spend much time in the apartment."

"I suppose." He turned his attention back to the apartment. "What channels do I get?"

"No idea," she said, not caring if she was abrupt. She watched as he went back inside. That was one thing no one had checked, television channels. She knew there would be something wrong with them. Stanley was a complainer. Since the airport, he'd had a list of minor complaints. They ranged from the length of time it took for the luggage pickup, to the hard seats in the rental van. The apartment was no different. It was too small, too little light, too... He was in the kitchen now, running a finger along the counter.

"What's around here? To do, I mean," Stanley said a few minutes later as he came up beside her. "Other than great scenery."

"You didn't research before you came?" She supposed he'd want to do something other than take pictures, but that wasn't her problem.

"Yes, but… I thought you might…" He smiled a slightly slick smile, obviously another ploy for her attention.

That was it.

"Have a seat," she said pushing him toward the couch just off the kitchen. She picked up a couple of brochures she'd seen resting in a small squat bookcase and tossed them at him. "Looks like you have some reading to do."

The way he didn't look at them. The way he dangled the brochures between his thumb and forefinger like they were tainted. All of it told her everything.

"You weren't really needing that information, were you?"

"No," he said, and blushed.

It was apparent that he'd only wanted a topic of conversation to connect with her. She didn't have time for conversation. That wasn't her job.

She turned and went back to the balcony, but made the mistake of looking over her shoulder. She sighed, feeling sorry for him and his rather hangdog expression. "Come here. Check out the view."

He stood a foot away from her. Unlike last time,

this time he looked at the scenery. There was an expression of awe on his face and she wasn't sure how he could have been so wrapped up in the apartment's conveniences, or lack thereof, to miss the extraordinary view the first time he'd stood on the balcony. But Stanley appeared to be a man with a one-track mind. He was no multitasker. Now he gazed out at the snow-covered plains and mountains that swept around the city limits seemingly transfixed, like he'd just realized all of this was here. He lifted his camera and snapped a picture then two, three... She lost count. Stanley was finally in his element and she was forgotten. Ten minutes later he put the camera down with a small smile on his face.

"Thank you," he said. "For picking me up. And putting up with me."

"It's what I'm paid for," she said, trying to inject a touch of humor into the words.

"I suppose."

"So what's with the name? Stanley, I mean," she asked.

He looked at her; his hazel eyes were awash in innocent confusion. At five-eight she almost looked eye to eye with him.

"I mean, it's a nickname obviously. How'd you get it? Did your parents come up with the name?" She wasn't overly interested. But it might serve to get to know the man she was supposed to protect just a bit better. Actually, it would help her get to know the man she would be chauffeuring around Wyoming. That was probably a more apt statement.

"No." He shook his head. "It was a name my older brother gave me. It's after a cartoon character. I don't suppose you have the program here. Anyway, I got the name when I was two. The show hasn't played in years. But at the time, he thought that I looked like the main character." He shrugged. "Of course, when he gave me the nickname, he was little more than a kid himself."

She wasn't sure what to say. How could they have missed the existence of a brother? The file listed no siblings. In fact, the closest relatives listed were an uncle and two first cousins. Then there were only distant relatives listed in order of succession. It was a major oversight, and it had her immediately concerned. "I didn't know you had a brother."

"I don't," he said rather sadly. "Not anymore. He died a few years before my mother." He cleared his throat. "Accident," he said with a rasp to his voice. "His death destroyed my parents."

For the first time, her heart went out to him. It was tragic, and he said it so nonchalantly. The hurt in his eyes told her that wasn't how he felt about the tragedy.

It was interesting how she'd had to tweak the profile she'd established for him. He was annoying but he wasn't arrogant; instead he had expectations. He was socially awkward, especially around the opposite sex. She wasn't sure if that was just her. The most surprising had been his compassion. There was a lot she still didn't know, as the file hadn't spoken to personality. But what she did know was that he was basically a good egg.

"Don't hit it!" he'd yelled when she'd swerved for an elk on the way from the airport.

"Oh my goodness," he'd said after the animal had dodged into the bush. "I'm so glad you did that. That you were able to swerve like that." He'd taken a slightly strangled breath as if he'd been holding it. "That he lived."

In that moment, she could have forgiven most of Stanley's annoying behaviors, at least the ones she'd recently suffered through, when he displayed that kind of compassion for a wild animal. Add in that he was the client, and they were never wrong, and he was in a pretty good place. For the first time she relaxed and smiled at him.

"I'm sorry," she said in reference to his brother. According to the file, his mother had died twenty-two years ago. His father had died a few years after that of a heart attack. She wondered what else the file might have missed.

"Don't be," he said softly. "He had a good life. Just short."

She looked at him with a frown. It was an odd thing to say about losing a brother, as far as she knew, his only sibling. Since it was accidental, she imagined it had been tragic—definitely sudden. She had questions, but she asked none of them. None of it was relevant to the case.

Instead she mulled over the strangeness of Stanley's response. Everyone dealt with grief differently, but she was curious. She started to say something and then stopped.

Before she could consider the matter further, there was a movement to her right. Her attention immediately focused on the cluster of stark, leafless trees on the edge of the parking lot. They were across the road, and her mind quickly calibrated the distance. Approximately one hundred feet to the right—shooting distance. She tensed, but her eyes never left that location.

"Go inside," she said over her shoulder. She wasn't taking any chances, code white or not. She could hear him breathing behind her. He wasn't listening, as usual. It was strange that they had a *usual* in the short time she'd known him. That was the one intriguing thing about him, despite his oddness—it was easy to develop a rapport with him. She shoved the thoughts back.

She focused on the change across the street, the potential threat. She doubted it was anything. But she wasn't taking the chance. She needed to focus on one thing, and that was keeping Stanley safe.

Something flashed across the street, like sunlight

on metal. She looked up. There was a break in the cloudy sky and a glimmer of sunlight.

With her Colt in her right hand, she moved close to Stanley, pushing him back with her left.

One sparrow, then two flew out of a low-lying bush that edged the parking lot. They flew diagonally down the street, the two joined by two more, as if they'd been disturbed.

"Get inside. Keep down," she commanded.

He looked at her, puzzled, his mouth working as if he were about to protest. She gave him another little shove when he continued to stand there.

It could be nothing. But she'd rather overreact and have Stanley safe. The other option wasn't worth considering. For that meant failure, and she'd never failed... The thought trailed off. Now all senses were on alert.

Something was off.

She peered over the balcony. The snow was lessening, but the wind was picking up. A stray fast-food wrapper was tagged by the wind. It seemed to skip across the street. She watched as it tumbled in the direction where, if she were to pinpoint trouble, she'd point there. But there was no evidence of anything. Just the same superficial signs and now nothing. The only noise was that created by the wind. The break in the clouds disappeared, and everything seemed dimmer.

She might have imagined it. The possibility was

high. She wasn't sure if there was trouble or not. What she did know was that her instincts screamed that something wasn't right. It was hard to pinpoint what had been the defining moment that had triggered her full attention. But now she was on and ready for action.

Seconds ticked by.

"What are you listening for?" There was a demand in his voice; it carried the edge of expectation, like someone who had always gotten his way.

A shot rang out, cutting off anything else he might have wanted to say. The glint of something, a glimpse of blue-black, a gun—or maybe that was just her imagination. The shot had been real. It seemed to come from exactly the spot she'd mentally marked as a potential problem area.

"Get down!" she shouted as Stanley let out a noise that sounded like a cross between a yip and a shriek. She hurled herself down and back so she was within range to take him down by force if necessary.

"What's going…" he began as she had him by the arm, taking him down, too.

"Shut up! Stay there!"

She got up in a half crouch while giving him a bit of a push on his chest to remind him to stay down. She turned her back to him, moving toward the railing. Cement, she thought with disgust. The railing was a solid block of cement. Great protection and lousy visual. The only way to find the perp was to make herself vulnerable and lift her head over the edge.

Another shot.

Seconds ticked by. A minute, then two.

A rush of movement to her right and a crash directly below her.

She was blinded by the balcony. She looked to her right. The ceramic planter that had sat on the railing had been taken out. It had crashed into the parking lot. Hit by gunfire, she was sure, considering everything that had happened in the last few minutes. But the sound had been muted and the only real alert was what had followed, the noise of pottery shattering. She bet that whoever was shooting at them was now using a silencer. Why hadn't he used it for the first shot or even the second? That was a mystery she might never have the answer to. Unnecessary question, unnecessary information, she told herself. But the shadow that flitted from one dead tree to the next and where the last shot had come from wasn't. This might be her only chance. She took aim and fired.

She glanced back. Stanley was on his knees in a position that in yoga was called a prayer position. The only difference was that his hands were covering his head.

She turned back to the balcony. She scanned the street. She doubted she'd hit anything. There'd been no evidence of her taking out anything more than the bark of a tree.

Whoever was out there would not want the attention of the sheriff. She had to assume that they would shoot only when they spotted a target, that they would not fire needlessly and create extra noise and, potentially, undue attention. She moved slowly, trying to find a place to see and not be seen.

Her Colt was clutched in both hands as she considered the next move. Everything had changed. The white-coded, dull little assignment had just been upgraded.

To code red.

# *Chapter Three*

"Why are they shooting at us?" Stanley looked at her as if the answer to that question would spin back the clock, as if this had never happened.

There was no time to ask who and why. No time for the volley of questions that answering that one question could turn into.

She looked over her shoulder. Stanley was crawling toward her. His face was white, but he wasn't stopping.

"Get back," Jade said, and waved him back toward the safety of the apartment. She should have known that there was a time limit on how long he'd follow instructions. She rose slowly to peer over the concrete railing. There was another movement to her right. A flash, and she dived down, glancing over her shoulder as she did so. Stanley hadn't moved.

"Stay down," she commanded in a whisper. "Stay there."

She shifted her attention away from Stanley.

The assailant might be across the street, but she had no idea if he was alone. She rose up on one knee. "This sucker's not done with us," she muttered as she peered over the balcony. Everything was quiet except for an odd shuffling sound behind her. She turned and found herself face-to-face with Stanley. "Down," she repeated, and he nodded, flattening himself to the balcony floor.

She hunched down, her eyes meeting his. Panic was in his eyes and in the tense line of his lips. "There's nothing you can do. This is why I was hired," Jade said patiently as if more words would somehow calm him. "You're unarmed," she reminded him, betting that he didn't even realize that important fact. She saw the fear in his eyes as she delivered the clinching words. "I'm not."

This time he seemed to get it as his frightened eyes met hers.

Jade turned, rising to her knees to peer over the balcony as she scanned the street for further trouble.

Silence.

To the left of the parking lot was a two-story plain brick building. Its main floor was boarded up. She looked away. Whoever had fired at them had done so from the right. That meant that they were close to the low-rise building. It was an office building, closed on the weekends. Nothing had changed from the last time she'd looked. She glanced back at Stanley. She breathed a sigh of relief to see that he had retreated inside. Her attention went back to the street. Her Colt was in both hands. There was no sound from the other apartments. Her mind went over the last few minutes.

Two shots.

Three if you counted the one with the silencer. That shot had been muted and mostly unheard by those inside, living in the vicinity, but it appeared, so had the others. Gunshots were out of the norm. They were sounds that many people might consider part of their imagination. Television programs, on-line games, the clamor of day-to-day living masked all sorts of noise, including that which was unanticipated and unfamiliar, gunfire. It would be easily discounted as part of the noise of a television program. Now there was nothing but a strange silence. Was the gunman still out there? And if he wasn't, where was he?

She slid down with her back to the concrete balcony railing. She debated whether now was the time to report in that her assignment had taken a critical turn.

One more check.

She pushed up over the balcony, looking left and right down the street. A movement to her left; she watched with bated breath. It was nothing but a jackrabbit that had made its way into the city. The hare took its time. It seemed to lope, hopping this way and that, stopping to sniff the air. Finally, it disappeared between two buildings. The street was again empty.

She sank below the railing as she put the Colt down and pulled her phone out of her pocket.

"Zafir," he answered with a concerned tone, for this number was never used except in case of emergency.

"Code red," she said simply. "I'm pinned down at the client's apartment. Shots from across the street at the client's balcony. The client's secure."

"Last count?"

"Unknown shooter. Three shots fired. Four, if you count mine. He has a silencer." She looked where the planter used to stand. "It's been quiet for over five minutes."

"Did you see…"

"Nothing," she interrupted. "No visual. Like I said, I got one shot in, that was it. I never had a clear shot and on a public street, well, that just made it difficult."

"I can imagine," he said. "Keep it contained if you can. I'll be there in five."

The call disconnected as abruptly as it had begun.

*Keep it contained if you can.*

With gritted teeth, she shoved the phone into her pocket. For a second she really wished that she could shove it somewhere else.

THE SNOW WOULDN'T stop falling. The man wiped perspiration and melted snow off his upper lip and swore as a car came down the street. Until now, it had been deserted.

He should have taken him out. Except he'd never had a clear shot. The woman had placed herself between him and his target. The plan was to take him out in a maximum of two shots and then get out before the authorities showed up. He'd already shot three. He couldn't fire any more. Even with his silencer, it was too dangerous. The woman was shooting back. Her gun didn't have a silencer. The cops could be alerted at any moment. His opportunity had slipped through his fingers, and Stanley had moved off the balcony. There was nothing to be done.

He looked at the handgun with disdain. It had failed him. The silencer didn't work as easily as he'd been told. He'd fumbled with it. As a result, he hadn't used it on the first two shots. The owner of the gun store had assured him that it was a "never fail." He'd said that it was easy to use. He had lied. If he were home, he'd go back and let him know what he thought of his lie. He couldn't. He was in a foreign country and he had to abide by its rules. If he stepped afoul of the law in any way other than planned, he had a greater chance of getting caught. That would destroy his chances at what was most important. But it was clear that taking someone out wasn't his forte. He needed help. He would find someone else, someone who could do the job for him.

He'd been stupid to think that he could remain

anonymous and complete the job. He needed the money. He hadn't come all the way here to fail.

He considered the fact that he required assistance. He wasn't sure why his cousin had hired him. Except that wasn't true. He knew why. Besides his lies and exaggerations and the fact that he really had killed before, he was disposable. He always had been. He grimaced.

Maybe a hit man was what he needed, someone more skilled at killing than him. He'd killed only two people in his life—one who had invaded his home and another who'd invaded his life. That hardly made him an expert, not like a hit man. He'd read of them and seen shows, American productions. Those shows had been fiction. Still, he knew that such people existed. They just did not advertise their wares in a storefront that was easily found.

He looked at the watch on his right wrist. He fiddled with the silver bracelet. It wasn't quite noon. He pulled out his phone and thumbed over the screen. There was one man who would know where to look. One man he could rely on to dig deep into the dregs of society and find someone who could do the job. The unfortunate thing of it was that it would not come cheap, and he needed every penny that had been offered him to get this job done.

Panic ran through him. He didn't have time to waste. He wasn't willing to give up on the money yet. He shoved the phone into his back pocket. He'd have to do it himself until, or unless, he found someone who was better. In the meantime, he was on his own, and he had less time than he'd anticipated.

His left leg ached from the cold and from having to scrunch into a cramped position for too long. The leg had plagued him since he was a child. It had been the result of what everyone had called an accident. He'd always known that it was no accident. Nothing that happened to him was accidental. The world was against him and always had been.

He rubbed his free hand along his calf as if that slight movement would dispel the bone-deep ache. His cousin needed to die, and he needed to do it soon. And if that meant he took out others with him, it didn't matter. What mattered was getting this job done and getting back to Morocco as soon as possible.

## Chapter Four

Zafir grabbed his keys, his go-bag and an extra magazine for his Glock and headed out the door. He hadn't expected to back anyone up. But every agent in the Wyoming office was busy and already assigned to a case. So there was no choice. He'd be stepping into the role of backup to Jade's lead. It was an exceptional situation, but it was also policy. He and Emir had hammered out the guidelines for Nassar Security a little less than a decade ago. Those guidelines had always included the brothers' full involvement. Action was what they loved. They'd vowed never to have that love drowned because of leadership duties and responsibility. They'd promised they'd be in the field whenever possible. Unfortunately, "whenever possible" had too often given way to days of tiring office duties. He was more than ready to move into action.

His hand brushed the gun. The solid feel of it seemed to connect with his hand in a way that was more an extension of him than the tool that it was. There was nothing more exciting than a new gun. Not even a glimpse of a spectacular woman or the chance to caress the sleek lines of the latest woman could compare—it was how he rolled. He didn't expect any of that would ever change.

Romance was short-term fun and long-term trouble. He'd grown up with parents in a loving marriage. Yet no matter how much he liked his future sister-in-law, Kate, he recoiled at the thought of his brother Emir marrying her. In case after case, he'd seen what jealousy and anger could do. Marriage and long-term relationships could be the perfect breeding ground for both those emotions. He wanted none of it, and he'd told himself that a long time ago.

He started the rental Nissan Pathfinder and was about to pop it into Reverse when his phone beeped. His hand dropped from the gearshift and he reached for it. Only a few numbers weren't screened out. He had two admin assistants to handle those calls that he didn't answer.

Emir's name showed on the screen. It wasn't a surprise. It wasn't uncommon for his twin to connect like this—unexpectedly. And as always, instinct had told him who it was before the first beep had finished.

"Yeah," he said, knowing he sounded rushed and hurried. This was a call he knew he couldn't miss, and even knowing that, the delay grated on him.

Something was up; Emir wouldn't have phoned otherwise. His twin didn't phone for social chats—never had, especially now, when their agency was overwhelmed and understaffed. It was something they'd have to address soon. His grip on the phone tightened.

"What's going on, Em?" he asked, trying to keep the edge from his voice. He knew that whatever information Emir had, it was going to put an additional crimp in his day.

"The code on your latest case just flipped to red," Emir said. Red meant that either the client's life was in imminent danger or there was a threat to an agent.

"I could have told you that five minutes ago," Zafir said, and his lips tightened. He didn't have a lot of time.

"What happened?" Emir asked.

"There were shots fired at the apartment we rented for the client. It's under control now. Jade held them off. Just one shooter that we know of. We're getting the client out of the area. Jade's waiting for me now." He dropped his hand from the steering wheel and rolled down the window an inch. A spatter of fresh snow hit his face. It was oddly calming. He loved the smell of fresh snow, but he was more anxious to get moving and make sure everything was secure.

"There's more to this than we were led to believe," Emir said. "It's making me uneasy."

The tension since he'd first answered the call retreated. He and Emir, as usual, were on the same page. But it had been the sudden change in status that he knew had really set him on edge. Moving into action always smoothed things over. "I'm at loose ends so I'll back Jade on this. What else do you have?"

"An explosion on an estate near Rabat belonging to your client's uncle." He paused. "The explosion was intentional. It was a homemade explosive device and it killed one of the estate's employees."

"Any idea who…"

"Of the bomber, nothing," Emir cut him off. "We believe he was acting alone. There was nothing left near the scene to even get a fingerprint. But even if there were," he mused, "whoever did it would have to have a criminal record for them to be of any use. One thing to consider, the uncle is old and very wealthy. I'd start digging into the details of that, but I'm buried in a case we have going here."

"I heard," Zafir said. "We're shorthanded with Faisal on the East Coast, and there's five other cases on the active roster. But we'll get it done. We always do."

He disconnected the call and looked at his watch. He debated getting in touch with Jade. Was the new information something that would change things for her in the next few minutes? He doubted that it would. But things could also change on a dime.

WITHOUT BACKUP, THE only thing Jade could do was keep Stanley safe and wait for Zafir to arrive. But one agent couldn't be in two places at once. They needed to get their client to a safe place. That was the priority.

She looked at her watch. They had to get moving and to find out who was after Stanley, and why.

She did a final sweep of the area. The street was silent. It had been like that for the last few minutes. She needed to make sure Stanley was safe. She stepped back into the apartment. She had to secure both him and the apartment before she went out and scouted a wider area. It was clear they needed to move him and for that they had to find a safe place. That wasn't her job. Her job was to protect him in whatever safe house was decided.

But when she stepped past the patio doors, the silence was heavy. She took a deep breath, trying to control her over-stressed breathing. The apartment was ominously silent except for the clock measuring off time; the steady beat made her want to yank it from the wall and chuck it over the balcony.

"Stanley!" Her gun was in both hands, aimed—ready. She took one step, moving left, her arms moving with her body, keeping the gun in front, ready. There was nothing to be ready for. The apartment was empty, and all that she could think was that it wasn't possible. She'd protected him, held off the sniper and made him safe, and now Stanley should be here waiting for her. As she moved through the small apartment she became more tense. It was clear that Stanley was gone, even his luggage was missing.

Outside a car door slammed.

She ran to the balcony, gripping the cold cement as she looked over the railing. The street was dreary, falling snow the only movement. She went to the other side, to the edge of the balcony that hugged the perimeter of the building. There, she could see into the parking lot and also see that the stall that her rental van had occupied was empty.

"Unbelievable," she said through clenched teeth. "Un-frickin-believable," she muttered. Nothing like this had ever happened to her. Until now, she could never have imagined it happening. So far she'd had a stellar, if short, career with Nassar—until now.

What had gone wrong?

How had this happened?

She'd handled the attack on the balcony smoothly only to lose the client. This didn't sit well with her, and it wasn't going to sit well with the agency. But it wasn't the agency she was thinking of, but rather the sinfully good-looking Zafir. She gritted her teeth. Instead of impressing him, which would up her chances of success and status with the company, she looked like amateur hour.

"Damn, Stanley," she gritted. "You're not making it easy to like you."

# Chapter Five

Jade headed out the door without a backwards glance. The apartment door banged behind her. She never checked if it was locked or not. It didn't matter. She wouldn't be back.

Irrelevant.

They needed to get moving. She had to brief Zafir. They needed to get wheels on the road and find Stanley.

As she stepped back into the parking lot ten minutes later, Zafir pulled up in an arctic-blue Pathfinder. Top of the line. She wouldn't have expected less. The metallic paint gleamed in the dull light. She'd had to wait for him, but she hadn't wasted any of that time. She'd gathered what evidence she could in the ten minutes it took Zafir to get here.

What she knew was that Stanley had been in a hurry. The evidence of that was a cover for one of his precious camera lenses, lying where the van had been parked. He was frightened, panicked even, but considering what had happened, she couldn't fault him. She ran the lens cover between her fingers.

Zafir stepped out.

"Stanley's gone," Jade said grimly.

He closed the driver's door. His gaze never left her face, and his eyes told her what he didn't. That he was waiting for her to fill him in.

"He took off while I was securing the balcony. No more than fifteen minutes ago." There was no sugar-coating the information. There was just getting it out and getting moving. "Took everything but his camera lens with him." She held it up with a look of irony. "He'll miss that." She stuffed it into her pocket.

"I don't believe this," Zafir said. A dark brow arched and his chiseled lips were flat, disapproving, as if this had all been her fault. "Foul play?"

"No. At least, I don't think so."

Silence beat between them, and with it, so many implications. Had she watched him closer, would this still have happened? Had she kept the keys for the van out of his reach, had she...

She met Zafir's troubled gaze. "There was no sign of scuffle. In fact, only one set of footsteps in the snow, and those are disappearing fast." She wiped snowflakes from her brow with the back of an un-gloved hand. "Tire tracks indicate he was heading west. They disappeared within fifty feet of his first turn."

Jade glanced to the street as if the van would miraculously appear. But there was nothing, no worn white van. If they didn't find him quickly, it would be too late. She knew that as surely as she knew that she'd had cereal for breakfast. Her stomach grumbled.

Her body was obviously not on the same page as her head. Now—there was no time for food. They had to get moving.

"I was on the balcony. He was in the apartment, or so I thought. He took the van while I was securing the area." She brushed a strand of hair off her face.

"He couldn't have gone far. There wasn't enough time," Zafir said. There was no inflection in his voice. There was no judgment, either. Somehow that made it all worse.

"You're right, and there's a chance he might return on his own. He's more than likely only frightened and has taken off to get away. Maybe he's thinking of taking some photographs. An hour or two in the countryside to calm his nerves." She shook her head. "Not going to happen," she said.

"It already has," he said, his lips compressed.

Now she could see the disapproval in his eyes.

She ignored that. It was true. Stanley had disappeared on her watch. But it was also true that she'd get him back, and then they'd move on to the next step, securing Stanley in another location. "Look, he's familiar with me. I can take your Pathfinder and retrieve him. You stay here in case he returns."

"No."

"No?"

"We'll go after him. Together."

"We?" Dread dropped into the pit of her stomach. That hadn't been what she planned even when she'd reported the code red. Somehow, she'd thought that she'd continue on in the case. Alone. That she'd keep Zafir informed as it progressed. That he'd assign another agent as backup.

"There's no one else available," he said as if reading her mind. There was a hard inflection in his voice that clearly told her this was nonnegotiable.

She took a breath. She was on edge, and it wasn't the situation. Zafir on paper was intimidating enough but in reality, even more so. She'd admired him for too long. Now she was scared that he was the one man who had the ability to pull her off her game. She took a deep breath. There were more important things to think of than her admiration for one of her employers.

She had to remember who he really was. He was a man like any other despite his legendary status with Nassar. She struggled with that, with staying focused on the job and not on him. But to her he was like no ordinary man. The cases he'd closed amazed her. She'd been in awe of what he had done, what he had faced and how he'd succeeded. She had to bring her adoration down to earth. Working with him had to be like working with any other man. She had no idea how to make that happen.

She took a breath and felt his dark eyes on her; the passion and intelligence in them was hot and commanding. She turned away. This was no time for such thoughts, and yet she had to allow them before she could discard them.

She had to remember that he was a womanizer, if office rumors were to be believed. For even now, he was looking at her with more heat than one would look at someone who was only a business partner. Worse, she wasn't immune.

Darn him, she thought.

"WHAT'S YOUR TAKE on Stanley?" His eyes drilled into hers and he knew that he probably seemed focused on her response like it was all that he had on his mind. He knew that it was all he should have on his mind. He needed to get his head in the game, for he found everything about Jade to be distracting. Her photograph, as he'd thought earlier, on first meeting her, hadn't done her justice. A photograph couldn't reveal biting intelligence or a body that was meant for...

*Outrageous*, his internal monitor roared at him. She was a gorgeous woman but more important, she was a business associate. The reminder wasn't much help.

His eyes went to her face. That was a safe place

to remain except for the fact that her eyes—her eyes were hypnotic, and her lips... She was muddying the waters of his normally clear mind worse than a sandstorm in the Sahara.

"He didn't seem to know how to act with a woman. I mean, he acted rather like a starstruck teenage boy rather than the middle-aged man he is. It was rather strange. Manageable, but strange." She looked at him and then followed everything she had said with a contradiction. "At least it was manageable, until now. I can't believe he's gone. I would never have expected that of him. He didn't appear to have that much initiative."

"He's frightened. Fear causes unexpected reactions." He felt nothing but empathy for the missing Stanley. He was probably intimidated by Jade's presence and likely knocked off his feet by her beauty. He bet that their client had been a mess before one shot had been fired.

He looked at Jade. Questions hung between them as well as the recently obtained intel that he needed to share. The rest of what happened, the explosion in Rabat, had the potential to impact this case. But it was information that would have to wait. First they needed to find Stanley. Then he'd tell Jade, and they could make some sense of it. He hadn't begun to analyze it himself. At this point, he had no idea if it impacted Stanley's presence here in the States or their ability to keep him safe.

"I should have remembered that. Fear," she repeated softly. "If I had, I might have prevented him from running," she said. "I should have checked on him before…"

"You didn't have time," he interrupted. "You were handling a potential assassin, which, by the way, was exceptional work."

"He got away."

"He didn't kill Stanley," he said. "That was your doing." He paused and scanned the street, which was empty, deserted as if the storm had confined everyone to their homes. "Was there a reason for anyone to try to take you out?" He was pretty sure of the answer to that even as he asked it, but he needed her to verify it.

"None," she said. "The shots stopped soon after I got Stanley out of sight."

"The threat was assessed wrong from the beginning," he said with a scowl, hating to admit any of that. He was on his phone punching numbers even as he talked. But that was how he ran things. His siblings joked about his ability to take multitasking to the next level.

"I've already called the rental agency," she said. "I mean, if that's what you're doing." Aggravation was thick in her voice. "They're activating the location device on the vehicle so that I'll have access."

Another sign that none of the glowing praise of her abilities had been wrong. The client had slipped away, but he was sure from the evidence presented, and what he knew of Jade, that it was through no fault of hers. His gut told him that nothing short of tying him down could have prevented it. But instead of telling her that, he scowled at her. Then he asked in a voice that would have suited any interrogation room, "You're sure he's planning to leave town?"

She nodded. "He's seriously into photography. As we knew from the file. But what we didn't know is how passionate he is. I don't think anything would stop him from taking the landscape pictures he came for. He's already made that clear. Add to the fact that he had a frightening experience, and that experience was in the city." She paused. "I suppose terrifying for someone unused to guns. He's comfortable in the countryside. He spends a lot of time there in Morocco."

She frowned.

"What is it?"

"You know, on the way here he asked me where the nearest international airport was. I told him that Casper was the largest and closest airport but you required a transfer for anything international. I didn't even get a chance to explain how limited the flight choice was. The whole topic was dropped because of the elk on the road. I managed to miss it and then we moved on to other topics."

"You think that's where he might be headed, Casper?" he said.

"No, at least not to hop a flight." She shook her head. "Despite the fact that someone tried to kill him, I don't think it was enough to have him heading home, at least not yet. For all his gaucheness, he has a stubbornness about him. Plus, he loves the States. He told me that this was the trip of a lifetime for him. I don't think he's apt to give up so soon. No, I think it's the opposite. Because of the extreme nature of the experience, he now thinks it's over. He thinks that he's safe. They tried and failed." She looked at him, her eyes seeming to graze his face with the passion of her commitment to this case. "Is that crazy?"

"Nothing at this point is crazy," he replied. "We've got to hit all angles, as you know."

"He mentioned Casper on more than one occasion as a drive he might like to take while he's here. There's some great photography between here and there."

"You don't…"

"I think—" she cut him off "—that he's taking that drive just a little earlier than planned." She shook her head. "I hope he's licensed and doesn't hurt himself in these conditions."

"We'll find him before that happens," Zafir said with gravel in his voice.

"I hope so," she said as she glanced at her phone messages. Her brow furrowed as her right hand ran through her hair. "The rental agency is having trouble with the app," she said. She put the phone down.

"It could be anywhere from a few minutes to an hour before they get it working." She frowned. "At least that's what the tech guesstimated in his message. In the meantime, they've pinpointed his last location, so that's hopeful."

There was something in the way that she looked at him that held some sort of warning. Yet his attention was fixated on her lips.

Pouty. It was an interesting and decidedly delicious feature, and it was completely distracting. He looked away.

"We don't have a lot of time. He's got a head start, and I don't trust him on his own. He could get himself killed left to his own devices for any length of time." There was an edge to her voice. "It's been too long."

"It only seems that way," he said calmly. It had only been minutes since his arrival, less than four to be exact.

He opened the driver's door of the Pathfinder as she got in the passenger side. As he shut the door, he went over what he knew. When he'd arrived, she hadn't looked directly at him. An admission of guilt. She believed the missing client was her fault. Now she met his look with the determination of a drill sergeant, raking over him, assessing. She'd accepted what she believed was her part in the situation and had moved on. She knew exactly what she was about and wasn't expecting any less from him.

Each case she'd been on, for one reason or another, had been the talk of the office on both sides of the ocean. They only hired the best. All their agents were cutting edge, yet in case after case her skills had shone above the others. In the fourteen months she'd been with the agency, she'd closed a record number of cases. She'd been lauded by two different municipalities and a women's group.

She pulled her Colt. She stroked the barrel like it was cherished and loved. But the way her focus remained on him sent a sensual shiver through him even when he realized that she was unaware of either the gesture or the suggestion loaded in it. She slid the weapon back into the holster at her waist.

He put the vehicle in gear.

"And what weapon are you going to use to contain Stanley when you find him?" he asked. He was curious about her, but prodding her for a reaction was a poor way to get information. He knew that, but it had slipped out, a question poorly timed and poorly formed.

"Excuse me?" She frowned, clearly unsure of what he was referring to.

"Got a peek at airport security footage. He's more of a handful than you're admitting." He shrugged as her frown deepened. "Of course, I did all that before you reported in. Just wanted to make sure everything was going all right."

"You were checking up?" Her face flushed, and

the words were tight, controlled, as if he had been doubting her abilities.

Her file mentioned a temper. It was information obtained from her psychiatric evaluation, required screening for all Nassar agents. In her interview, she'd admitted to an impoverished blue-collar, single-parent upbringing. As a result of that, she'd declared she had high goals and expectations for herself. She'd proven that ambition and ability again and again in the field. It was only her quick temper that might cause her to stumble along the way. So far it had proven to be well controlled. She'd mastered even that.

"Actually, at the time I was just briefing myself, in case you needed backup. Which…" His eyes met hers, stormy blue and almost accusatory. "Turns out you do. The case is upgraded and the client has disappeared, has he not?" They were harsh words that held none of his admiration. Instead they were fighting words. He needed any doubts she felt to be replaced by a driving will to succeed.

Silence hung between them for a second, two.

"It could have happened to anyone," she said with an edge to her voice.

"Right," he agreed. "But it happened to you." He couldn't help pushing the envelope, seeing what her reaction would be.

He knew she was annoyed. His last comments were uncalled for, insensitive if you didn't know where he was going with them. He might have pushed her too far; he reined it in. "I'm sorry."

Her lips were compressed and the look in her eyes suggested she'd rather see him in hell than here, and she wasn't much interested in his apology.

"Look, on this case I'm no one's boss. I'm sorry for giving that impression or for laying blame when none should be." He cleared his throat. He needed to eat crow to make this case go smoothly. "I was a jerk."

"Agreed," Jade said with a hint of a smile. "Let's go," she said. "We need to find Stanley."

# *Chapter Six*

"We've got a location," Jade, said looking up from her phone.

"Still moving?" He turned the corner.

"Yes…no. Unbelievable!" She shook her head.

"What's going on?"

"I've lost the feed." She turned the rental's locating app off and then back on. She smacked her palm against the dash. "Off-line again. I can't believe it. What are the odds of that?"

Neon lights glared to her right. A convenience store. Ahead of them, a Jeep turned off a side street. There was no sign of the white van, nothing that said Stanley had even been here.

"Exactly," Zafir said with a small laugh.

"Slow down," she said, and instead he seemed to speed up as her shoulder hit the door and the seat belt tightened, easing the impact as he took a curve in the road too fast and the vehicle slid.

He glanced at her with a look of apology and

slightly raised eyebrows, as if he were hinting that it might be a joke. This was no time…

The thought was broken. A siren flashed and bleeped, once, twice. Zafir slowed down and pulled over.

"Unbelievable," she muttered. There'd been enough delays. Stanley could be in any kind of danger by now. There was the possibility that they weren't the only ones on Stanley's tail. The earlier assailant could be tracking him, too.

"We'll make this quick," Zafir replied. "It's Jake," he said as he glanced in the rearview mirror.

"This case just won't catch us a break," she said as they waited for Jake to approach. The agency had a silent agreement in place with local law enforcement. It allowed them reasonable leeway to operate—the occasional bout of speeds slightly over the limit were usually overlooked. With any luck, they'd be on their way in minutes. Still, minutes were minutes.

She looked back at the police unit and down at the app, which was now showing Stanley's progress. "He's moving," she said. Of all times to be pulled over, just when the rental agency had fixed its software glitch. She looked at her watch and back at the app. "He's got a ten-mile lead on us."

"Jake," Zafir said, acknowledging the sheriff as he came up to the window.

"We're on the lookout for your sniper," Jake said with a curious look inside the vehicle.

Jade frowned. She was unsure how the sheriff would have learned of the incident so quickly. There were no witnesses that she knew of and she hadn't reported it. No witnesses—was that a false assumption?

"I would think that if you leave town, he'll leave with you," Jake said. He glanced past Zafir and took her in with an appreciative sweep of hazel eyes.

Jade tensed and bit back what she thought of the sheriff's unspoken admiration. It wasn't the first time she'd met up with the man and not the first time he'd offered that type of response. It was unprofessional and made her want to smack him, both times. She bit back the words, and her right hand reached for her Colt. The smooth feel and the power it promised were always soothing, no matter what the emotion.

"There's a weather warning. Travel isn't advised," Jake said drily.

"We don't have much choice," Zafir replied.

Snow fell on the windshield. The wipers beat a slow dance. The snow, the wipers, Jake's slow mannerism, all of it beat like the ticking of a clock, reminding them that they were wasting time.

Jade looked out the passenger window. *Hurry up*, she thought.

Jake wasn't the most ambitious sheriff they'd ever had. He was probably thanking the stars or the universe or both that the case was out of his hands. That attitude often made things easy for the agency, but it didn't give any of them a reason to respect the man.

"I suppose you don't," Jake agreed. "I'll keep my eyes peeled here."

Jade grimaced at his words and at the second almost-lecherous look he gave her.

"Thanks," Zafir said, and glanced at her with a smile that said he knew her pain.

She offered him a weak smile.

Zafir nodded and put the Pathfinder in Drive, pulling away from the curb and away from Jake. The police car sat where they had been pulled over, the emergency lights still flashing.

All in all, they'd wasted less than five minutes.

"There's a coffee shop just around the corner. I'd put odds on Jake making an appearance there now that his services aren't needed." He shook his head. "Remind me if I need to cloud an issue with Jake to send you in."

"That wasn't even funny," she said with a smile.

"No, I suppose it wasn't."

"He's the most laid-back sheriff we've ever had. Guaranteed to do nothing," she said. "He's not even interested in the issue. Just how he can get out of work."

Zafir laughed. It was a low, almost sexy growl that curled down her spine with a seductive caress. "Good thing there isn't too much going on in Jackson."

"Yeah, not too much at all," she said with irony in

her voice. She thought of the earlier sniper and of all the cases that Nassar had quietly worked under the nose of local law enforcement. It had been different once, the law more involved, or so her colleagues told her. That had all been before her time.

Five minutes later they hit the city limits. Her finger ran along the route indicated on the app. "Where the heck is he going?" Jade muttered. "He's traveling back roads, keeping off the interstate. But there's miles to go on that road before there's a more trafficked road." She ticked off the miles on her fingers. "Too many miles of vulnerability. What is he thinking?"

"I'd assume, from what I know, a lot of panic," Zafir said. "I really don't think it's about photographs at this point."

"Whatever his reasons, this is crazy." She shook her head. "We've got no idea what or who else is out there."

Zafir gunned the Pathfinder as they left the city limits. But this wasn't the interstate, and it wasn't made for fast travel. The highway was slick, narrow and plagued by antelope straying onto the road. The animals unexpectedly crossed the highway during the dawn and dusk hours, and sometimes in between. It was all unpredictable.

"You might want to slow down," she said. "We don't want to die like…" She stopped. Motor vehicle tragedies, death—loss, all of it—the possibility that life could be short. All Nassar employees had been brutally reminded in a recent case. The case exposed a decade-long cover-up.

"In an accident," she finished lamely. "Could you slow down? Just a bit. The antelope, the snow… It takes one misstep…"

"Do you want Stan to live or die," he growled.

He gripped the wheel and looked at her with anger in his dark eyes.

She realized then that he'd known what she had been referring to. He recognized exactly what she'd been backtracking over—his parents' fatal accident.

"I'm sorry," she said.

"Don't be," he said. "It was a long time ago."

He gripped the wheel. But the look he gave her seemed like a challenge. There was a charge in the air, an awareness of each other that was different, more pronounced, than it had been before.

Her phone beeped. It was nothing more than a reminder of the passing of time.

"Dang it!" Stanley muttered as the van slipped into a skid and he wrestled with the wheel. The vehicle didn't respond. The slide continued as if the van wanted to fling itself sideways on purpose. It was unstoppable.

He gritted his teeth and hit the brakes. The van rocked as its tires spun, and the slide seemed to increase in speed rather than decrease. He was heading for the ditch and there was no stopping it.

He turned the wheel—nothing. The van was on a mission of its own. This shouldn't be happening. He knew what to do; at least he thought he had. Snow in the mountains of Morocco wasn't an uncommon occurrence, but he'd never driven in it. In fact, he'd never driven in Morocco, period.

He vaguely remembered that hitting the brakes wasn't a good idea. He tried to steer, but which way? Into or out of the slide. The advice he'd read was lost.

His heart pounded. Coming here had been a bad idea, and he'd known it would be from the beginning. It was a feeling he'd had on the flight over. Now the feeling was a reality. It had been a mistake. All of it, coming here—running from Morocco, running from Jade. He wasn't sure where to begin, where to unravel it to make it all right. He gripped the wheel. He remembered something about turning into the skid. Was that right?

He turned the wheel, but even if it made any difference at all, he was too late. The van rocked and then slid off the road, wobbling like it would tip over before it lurched to a stop in the ditch, stopped by a bank of snow.

Stanley stayed where he'd been thrown. His chest was pressed against the steering wheel. He took a breath and then another. He was still alive, and as he became more aware, he realized that a horn was honking.

It was his horn.

He leaned back. The honking stopped.

He put the van into Reverse, and the tires spun. The van didn't move even as the engine revved. He put it into Drive. The same thing.

Nothing.

"What were you trying to do?" he muttered to himself. He'd wanted peace and quiet. Jade had flustered him, and the attack had terrified him. He hadn't planned to be gone long. In fact, he'd only wanted to take a few pictures. When he'd come here, to Wyoming, all he'd wanted was peace. Instead, he'd been saddled with a gorgeous type-A-personality woman. She made him jittery. She reminded him of a time when he'd almost had a nervous breakdown. He'd been a child, but the feelings had been real. He'd hated his life, his home. It wasn't like that anymore.

Home. He wanted to go home. This had been a mistake.

He'd told Prince Rashad that protection on his trip was unnecessary. He'd insisted on it. He'd been wrong.

He didn't know why anyone would threaten him. He'd done nothing, had nothing. That was all going to change, but it wasn't enough for someone to kill him. The trust fund would end if he died. So why would someone shoot at him?

His phone beeped as if it had been listening, as if it somehow had the answer. He pulled it out and checked the text message, praying that it was Jade.

Except it couldn't be, for she didn't have the number, didn't even know of the phone.

His hands shook, praying for salvation. But the words he read were some of the most terrifying of his life. He was reading the words of a ghost, a demon who was, and always had been, out to get him.

He held the phone clutched against his sweaty palm. He couldn't let it go. He was mesmerized. There should be no text. No one had the number except for his uncle. He'd left the information for him on a table in the small cottage on his uncle's estate. It was the cottage where they'd spent many pleasant afternoons playing rummy and drinking tea. He'd bought the phone solely for this trip so that he could keep in touch with the animal rescue that was his passion, and his uncle, who was his responsibility. Until now, it was unused.

For a minute, two—he couldn't move. He thought about what was on that phone. Nothing. They were meaningless words. He took a deep breath. It was a lie. They weren't meaningless words; they were the words that foreshadowed every nightmare he'd had as a child.

He gripped the wheel. He needed help, and there was no help here. He was on his own. He had to save himself.

He took a deep breath. He should never have run, but he'd also needed time to get himself together.

"So, get it together," he muttered through gritted

teeth as he dropped his hands into his lap. He was in a bad situation, and it was his own stupid fault. Now he had to get himself out. He just wasn't sure how or what he needed to do. Should he lie low for a while? If this was a scene from one of his favorite movies, that's exactly what the actors would do.

He stroked his camera and shrugged his jacket on. Despite his thoughts, he didn't know what he was going to do. Everything had changed with that text. He wasn't sure what it meant, and he knew he didn't want to think about it. He looked at the map he'd lifted from the apartment. There was a small community five miles north of the last intersection. He could disappear into the wilds of Wyoming for a while, until he figured out what to do.

He slipped out of the van. Snow had stopped falling but still the drifts were high enough for snow to fall over the tops of his sneakers. Too late, he realized that he should have listened to Jade and purchased boots. Of course, even if he had listened, there had been no time to shop. He turned around and grabbed his camera, ignoring the cold trickle that ran down his ankles. He'd have to endure that discomfort.

He pulled the phone out of his pocket. He looked at the message again. He couldn't help it. No matter how disconcerting it was, he felt like none of it was real. The dead didn't come back to life, but the message suggested they did.

No one ever said those words. For they were

strange words that no one would say or had said in the context of most communication. No one but his brother had used those same words to torment him and to torment the animals he loved so well. But his brother was dead.

He shivered, unsure of what it all meant.

He looked at the message one more time before he threw the phone. He watched as it sank into the snow-covered ditch. He was left with only a memory and the knowledge that the dead really can come back to life.

For the first time since he'd last seen his brother, he felt the urge to hit something. But violence wouldn't fix anything; he'd learned that a long time ago.

He walked, or more aptly, he slogged through the snow. He kept going long past where the van had been left. Finally, at the edge of the ditch, he bent down to crawl through the barbed-wire fence. He headed across the field. It was the shortest distance to the town on the map that he'd just stuffed into his pocket.

He felt oddly exhilarated. The horror was behind him. He was taking charge of his own life.

Everything was so silent, so still and so white. It was pristine, gloriously wild and untouched. He took a deep breath of air so clean that it made him shiver and want to hug himself with joy. This was how the world should be—innocent, beautiful and safe. He raised his camera to create a memory of the moment. He took one picture, then two. The camera click was the only sound in the pristine silence.

Minutes passed.

Leaving had been right, he was sure of it now as he aimed and clicked—repeating over and over...

The first gunshot had Stanley diving face-first into the snow. Minutes ticked by. Gingerly he lifted his head. He was five yards away from a shanty. It wasn't much. The weather-softened gray wood looked like it might tumble down with a slight breeze. He had been intrigued by it only seconds earlier. He already had a half dozen photos of it. Right now it was all that stood between him and imminent death.

Jade was gone.

Prince Rashad had been right. He needed protection. It wasn't safe anywhere. He'd been right, but he'd been right for all the wrong reasons.

He could do this. He had to do this; there was no one else but himself to depend on, to get away from the madman who was trying to kill him.

Another shot sheared a drift of snow only ten feet away from him.

A man shouted. The words were as indistinguishable as they were angry and threatening.

Bile rose in his gut, and he fought to keep from throwing up. He couldn't think about the past or about what the future might bring. He had to deal with the now. He had to stay alive.

He crawled the remaining feet to the shanty. Then he stood up and bolted through the doorway, pulling the broken door closed behind him. He couldn't move another step. Instead, he dropped to his knees. Huddled in a ball, his camera dangling around his neck, he considered how he could escape from this new insanity.

# Chapter Seven

"The van's not moving," Jade said with a scowl. She shook the phone as if that would change what the app was telling her. "I thought the app had stalled out again. But that's clearly not the case. The van just isn't moving." She paused and looked at him. Her delicate brows were drawn together. "I don't think it's on the road, either, but I can't bring up a real-time photo."

"What are we looking at?"

"Eight miles," she said. "So less than ten minutes and we'll have our answer."

"With any luck," he said drily.

They drove in silence. The snow had finally stopped falling. Here and there, gold shocks of prairie grass burst through the snow. A herd of antelope grazed a half mile to their right, halfway between the foothills and the road. Snow-capped mountains were visible in the distance. At another time, under other conditions, it would have been a scenic route.

"There's either a problem or it's as simple as he stopped to take pictures." She squinted as if that would somehow bring their client into view. "It makes sense. He probably isn't feeling threatened. He feels safer out here. Like he left all the danger behind." She paused. "I'm just speculating, but from what I know of him…"

"He's impulsive."

"Big-time." She looked out the window and back down at the app. The van still hadn't moved. She wondered if Stanley was still with the vehicle. She hoped so. "We might find the van, but there's no guarantee that he's still with it."

That possibility hung between them. Neither of them mentioned the other possibility, that Stanley was already dead. It was an option of which they were both aware but one that neither of them was willing to entertain.

"This case isn't going to be like any other we've had." He broke the silence as he glanced at her. "It's the first to become transcontinental."

"What do you mean?"

"Emir called just before we left." He navigated an icy patch on the road before looking her way again. "I would have told you immediately, but as you know, we were short of time and we had other priorities."

"What do you have?" she said, and couldn't stop the hint of impatience in her voice.

Hot air blew in from the vents, and snow dusted and swept across the road in seemingly chaotic swirls.

The highway was becoming even more treacherous as the snow that had melted on the pavement turned to ice when the temperature plummeted.

"There was an incident reported in Rabat, Morocco, three days ago. A cottage on the grounds of an estate was blown up. A gardener died."

"Wow," she muttered. "How is that tied…" She broke off before her thought could even become a full question. Her gut told her that the case was about to be turned on its head.

"What was destroyed was a cottage that Stanley apparently likes to retreat to. He often spends time there with his uncle playing cards." He looked over at her. "The estate belongs to his uncle."

"You're kidding me," she said, and she couldn't keep the edge out of her voice. She shook her head. "No, obviously you're not. I can't believe this."

He glanced at her, a frown on his face. "We didn't hear anything until early this morning."

"And it took this long to tell me? And the case wasn't upgraded," she said. She was beginning to fume. Not only had the code not been changed until they'd been shot at, but she hadn't been told earlier.

"It was reported to Emir," he said, mentioning his twin and head of the Marrakech branch. "The connection with Stanley wasn't made until just before I left to meet you."

The Pathfinder skated for a moment over a patch of black ice. A minute passed and then two before he spoke again.

"The results of the explosion didn't even make Moroccan news. Stanley's uncle has pull."

"How'd Emir find out?" Her hand relaxed and dropped from her waistband where her gun was concealed. It was an instinctive reaction to danger, perceived or otherwise.

"Our family's employee grapevine."

"Your employees? The ones who work on the family estate?"

"Exactly. The Marrakech estate employees are sometimes our strongest communication device for homegrown cases. This time, one of our maids had a sister whose friend worked at Stanley's uncle's estate."

He offered her a lopsided smile. "Emir went to the mansion as soon as he heard and interrogated the uncle. According to Emir—to quote him, 'he's old, but a crusty bugger.' Apparently, he's an army vet and wasn't intimidated by much, but Emir has a knack about him. If there's information to be had, send in Emir. He's the human bulldozer."

The news of the explosion was unexpected, and she knew, with the connection to Stanley, that it had the potential to change everything they'd thought about this case. She waited for him to continue.

"We're swamped. There's not an available agent

on either side of the Atlantic. Emir could only do so much with his time constraints. It's our case, so he's left the rest up to us."

"Anything else?" She thought of the implications, of the possibility that this might end overseas. She swallowed back the exciting challenge of an overseas case.

"The gardener who died in the blast was a new hire. He had no connections to the family. His credit rating was clear—no debt, no grudges that could be found."

"No threat to anyone. Wrong place, wrong time." It was such a common occurrence as to be trite, almost clichéd. Expect the Unexpected was a motto that few people lived by and more should. It was a motto that was almost a religion to her.

"Exactly. But so far we're basing everything on assumption. But it did flush something else out. The uncle obviously has money, and he's a widower. More importantly, he's just updated his will. The new beneficiary is none other than Stanley."

"Stanley?"

He nodded. "It's so recent and been kept so quiet that even Stanley may not know."

"This is crazy," she said. "So Stanley stands to inherit what I assume may be a fortune."

"That's what we have for now. But…"

"You think there's more," she interrupted. This was going south fast.

"Yes." He looked at her with a hint of admiration with an overtone of surprise. "As you know, we've continued a low-key investigation in Morocco into Stanley's background. It's been hampered by a lack of resources. My sister, Tara, will be helping out part-time with the online investigation."

"Computer science is her major," she said. "Perfect fit."

She smiled hearing what he wasn't saying—that Tara's involvement in the business was safe. Tara was Zafir's youngest sibling and only sister. Only months ago she'd been the victim of a kidnapping. Since then, her brothers wanted to keep her safe by sheltering her. But their sister's formidable will was well known throughout the agency. It looked like that will had won out. Jade thought, from everything she knew of Tara, that she'd make a fantastic agent once she finished her schooling. She was smart enough to know not to mention such an idea to Zafir.

"So, Stanley's inheritance, how much are we talking—enough to put his life in danger?"

"More than enough. Around fifty million or so American dollars. That's what Stanley's uncle admitted to Emir," Zafir said. "From what Emir told me of the estate, he's probably not exaggerating."

She shook her head.

"And Stanley..."

"Like I said, Emir was fairly certain that Stanley was in the dark about the whole matter."

"If he knew, I don't know if he could keep it a secret long." Or could he, she thought, thinking of the Stanley who had stolen her rental and bolted. He wasn't as open or as naive as he liked to portray. "So who wins if Stanley is taken out?"

"That's the burning question," he said. "Is it enough motivation to take him out?"

"It's fifty million," she said with disbelief in her voice. "I don't know about your world, but in mine that's a crazy amount of money."

"Which means it's enough to kill for."

"Exactly. Can you step it up a notch?" She heard the edge in her voice. "I know, first I tell you slow down and now I'm telling you to speed up. Kind of contradictory."

"You think?" he asked.

"I know it's slick." She shook her head. "I know—weather conditions. Of all times to get a late storm. Hopefully, Stanley manages these roads. Last thing we need…"

Her words dropped off, for they both knew the other concern. Accidents on days like this were not uncommon. Toss in a traumatized foreigner and the odds just skyrocketed.

Zafir glanced at her with a smile and a slight arch of his dark brow. "We'll get this case roped in and under control," he said. "Weather, assassin, whatever we have to tackle. We've both seen worse."

"We need to know the wording of that will," she

said. Her mind was already moving ahead to other issues. "And next of kin, including those not listed."

She looked at him with a half smile, but she clutched the door handle and squinted into the horizon. She saw what they'd both been looking for—the white flash of metal paint. They'd found the van. But it was also what they were hoping not to see, for the van was in the ditch and from this distance there was only the van in sight. So where was Stanley?

# Chapter Eight

Zafir hit the brake and brought the Pathfinder to a stop on the edge of the highway. The sun had broken through minutes earlier and the snow had stopped over ten minutes before that.

Jade had her Colt in both hands. She'd put a bulletproof vest on before they stopped. Now, like her, he made a visual scan of the area before approaching the van.

He adjusted the vest, shifted his grip on his gun and moved in just behind Jade. Big mistake. She had a butt more attractive than any agent's should be. He pulled his gaze back to the perimeter around the van. He crept up beside her. The side of the van nearest the field was sunk lower than the rest, the hood dipping into the ditch. The right front tire was flat. The driver's door was half open as if the driver had exited in a rush. They split up, Jade approaching that side while he moved to the passenger door and pulled it open. It took a good heave to do it. He frowned. The van was old. It should have been moved off the lot rather than rented. Yet in an odd way it had been the perfect vehicle. Plain and unobtrusive, it blended.

The van was empty except for the Wyoming tourism magazine that lay open to a page with a map of Wyoming. A half-eaten candy bar lay beside it and in the back was Stanley's suitcase, duffel and his camera bag.

"He ran," Jade said with that soft-as-butter tone to her voice. She straightened, looking across the field as if seeing immediate danger there. But there was nothing. "Let's hope he didn't get far." Her lips pinched as she looked at the van and back again at the landscape.

She looked down.

"What the…" She moved a few feet from the van and reached down to pick up a disposable phone. It was the kind bought in convenience stores for short-term use.

She flipped it open. "I don't think it's ever been used," she said after she scanned through the call history. "Wait, no, there's a text. Number isn't registering." She frowned. "Doesn't make much sense."

She handed it to him.

"'By your ears.'" He frowned. The phrase was odd and she was right, made absolutely no sense. "I'm not sure what the hell that's supposed to mean if anything." He handed it back to her, and she shoved it into her pocket.

"It's too strange not to mean something," she said with a frown.

"We'll take a closer look at it later. We don't have time to speculate."

He moved along the road, a few feet from the van. He was searching for evidence that there'd been any other vehicle involved. There was nothing. Everything seemed to end here, with the van.

He bent down, his ungloved hand sweeping across the snow as he looked at the footprints.

"Sneakers."

"It was what he was wearing when I picked him up at the airport," she said.

He looked back at her and saw she was squinting. The sun was overly bright against the snow. He'd grabbed his sunglasses before they'd left the vehicle. She lowered her sunglasses, which had been perched on top of her head.

"He must have been terrified," she muttered.

And without explanation, he knew that she was revisiting that earlier moment on the balcony of the first safe house.

"I should have been on him immediately. Instead, I gave him a window," she said with a touch of self-recrimination.

"You were securing the perimeter. Critical work. You couldn't have been two places at once."

"And Stanley disappears on my watch," she said grimly. She held up a hand. "Don't say anything more. The results are the same. It was my watch. You can't deny that." She looked around, scanning the area. "I need to take responsibility so I can fix what didn't work. So I can make sure it doesn't happen again."

"It could have happened to any one of us," Zafir said.

"Doesn't make me feel any better," she said.

"You wouldn't be as good as you are if it did."

He looked along the ditch, following the sneaker prints as far as he could from where he stood. "Let's go," he said.

She took the lead. He followed as she walked along the ditch, following Stanley's footprints. They'd walked for about a quarter of a mile before the footprints veered into the field.

"No trespassing," she muttered as they approached a metal sign attached to the fence. "Great."

They ducked under the barbed-wire fence and headed into the field, disobeying the sign, following Stanley.

"Look," she said a few minutes later.

In the distance there was a dilapidated small building.

"A homesteader's cabin?" she asked.

"Possibly."

They walked in silence for another few minutes. In other circumstances, it would have been a beautiful walk. Another minute passed and then two as they made their way through the isolated ranch land.

The rotting remains of a shanty that looked like nothing more than one room stood about another half mile ahead of them.

"Do you think he's there?"

He shook his head. "We couldn't be that lucky."

Scrub brush to their left was laden with snow. Silence seemed to wrap around them.

Despite what he'd said, the footprints seemed to be leading directly to the shanty.

"Where is he going?" Jade muttered. "He could take pictures anywhere around here if that's what he wants."

His gaze swept over the land immediately around them. The ground was frozen, but the promise of spring seemed to burst through the snow. A stalk of wild barley here, a green bud there. It was all beautiful and oddly surreal.

"If he's there, we're close enough for him to hear us," Jade said. "I'll call him."

Before she could act on it, there was a flash to their right.

They looked at each other. Ahead of them and just to the right of the shanty there was a dip in the land before it rose into foothills. It was the perfect place for an ambush.

Gunfire echoed through the valley and had them flat on their bellies.

Jade turned her head, her cheek to the ground. "What the hell?" she murmured. "I didn't expect that."

"Leave me alone!" came a voice from just ahead of them, very near, if not in, the shanty.

"Stanley," she mouthed.

"Son of a…" Zafir said through clenched teeth as Stanley screamed something incomprehensible. "Is there any way we can get him to quiet down before he gets himself killed?"

"Or us," she muttered.

Another shot ricocheted off a stand of barren poplars that clustered on the south side of the little structure. This time they could judge the position of the shots. They originated from somewhere behind and to the right of the shanty.

Jade motioned to her left. There was another grove of trees there.

He nodded. It was best if they came in from two different angles.

"If I head for the trees, I can divert him, maybe get a look at what we're dealing with."

"Keep low," he whispered. "For whatever reason he's not shooting directly at us. Yet he had to have seen us." He wondered at that.

"We're trespassing. He just wants to frighten us. It could be as simple as that," she whispered.

He nodded. "Don't shoot unless necessary," he whispered. "Let's try to get a handle on what's going on. If it's a rancher, we don't want to appear aggressive and get Stanley killed."

She nodded and moved away, almost doubled over as she kept low to the ground.

He knew that Jade would come in on the shanty from the left. She would work her way through the dips and hollows in the land. He was sure of her ability to keep herself out of the sniper's line of vision. There was plenty of brush now that they were almost into the foothills that she could use for cover. He was going straight in, using the rockier, hilly face ahead of him. He wasn't sure how they were getting Stanley out. But a gunfight was the last option.

Another shot.

He moved forward and saw red plastic sticking out of the snow. A shotgun shell.

Was it possible that they were being shot at by someone armed with a shotgun? Or was the shell just the remnants of an earlier hunting party and nothing to do with their current situation.

Who was shooting and why? The earlier shots in town had been from a handgun, at least that's what they had assumed. A shotgun wasn't easily hidden and not usually the weapon of choice in an urban environment.

He pushed the thoughts away. Now wasn't the time to build the profile, rework what little they had or think about it at all. He needed to keep Jade safe and then ensure Stanley was protected. He didn't think much about the fact that he'd just put the client last in his priorities.

He looked to his left. There was nothing. Everything was still. His heart stopped. Had she been hit? Was she hurt? He began to move closer to the shanty. He was on his knees and elbows, trying to keep his Glock out of the snow and his head down.

Jade had slipped out of his line of vision. He didn't like not knowing exactly where she was.

He scanned the landscape looking for movement. There was nothing, only silence.

The door to the shanty creaked open.

His grip on his gun tightened and his teeth gritted. Stanley needed to close the door, and if thoughts could direct him to do so, he'd do it now. Amazingly, the door closed.

Zafir's attention veered as a movement to his right stole his attention. A shot, then two. Snow and dirt kicked up near him.

Cease-fire was off. Whoever was out there was now directly shooting at them. Threatening them with deadly harm.

He fired in the direction the shots had come from. But he still had no visual. There was a shout from the shanty, or it could have been a shriek. He wasn't concerned. From the information he had on Stanley it might be fear. He doubted that Stanley was injured, because none of the shots had hit the shanty.

Jade slipped down beside him.

"I had a visual. Just a glimpse. Male—wearing a green-and-brown hunting cap, and he has a shotgun."

"Local?"

"Possibly," she said. "I can't see a sniper using a shotgun."

He nodded. She was right about that. He'd thought the same when he'd found the shell.

"Who are you?" he shouted.

"Get the hell off my land!" came the low, gravelly voice.

"Jade!" This time the frightened voice was Stanley.

"Stay there, Stanley!" Jade shouted as she glanced at Zafir.

Another shot echoed through the valley, seeming to bounce off the hills.

"Cease-fire!" Zafir shouted. "We'll move off, but our friend needs help. Let me get him and we'll be gone."

His request was met by silence.

Zafir moved forward, using a bush a few feet ahead of his previous position for cover. Now he could see the green-and-brown low-brimmed hat poking over a boulder forty feet to his right.

"Nassar Security," Zafir yelled. "Our client is an amateur photographer. He just wanted to get some pictures. He didn't know he was trespassing."

"This is private land!" the man shouted back, as

if that was all that mattered and any explanation was null and void.

"He's Moroccan, a foreigner. He didn't know to read the signs," Zafir yelled back. There was a time when property was the most valuable thing a man owned on these windswept plains. That need to protect it was still very much alive. Stanley had unsuspectingly stepped from one bad situation into another.

"He isn't fluent in English. It isn't his first language," he added as if that might make any difference. It was a lie, but it served a purpose in their current situation. He knew Stanley could read, write and speak English perfectly, as well as Arabic and French. It wasn't uncommon for educated Moroccans to be multilingual. He could only guess which one was his primary language.

He waited.

Silence.

He looked back at Jade. Her lips were tight, and she looked worried.

A minute passed, and then two.

"Drop your weapons and put your hands up!" the throaty voice demanded.

The command was unprecedented. The situation was unexpected. None of it was fitting anything that had transpired before in any other case.

"I'll put my gun away," Zafir said to Jade as he slid his gun into his holster and nodded to Jade to stay where she was. He wasn't going to put both of them at risk. He was fairly certain that they'd been cornered by an enraged rancher. With any luck, his compliance would diffuse the situation.

He put his hands up.

"The client is unarmed," he said. "I'm from Nassar Security," he repeated. "I'm an investigator. State licensed," he added, in case that hadn't been clear, and in case the man hadn't heard of them or their reputation. "I'm hired to protect the man in your shanty." He repeated the fact as if it explained everything: "He's unarmed."

He was taking a risk, but now he was almost certain the risk was minimal. He had a gun in the back of his belt that he could reach, and Jade had him covered.

"If you're who you say you are..."

"I am," Zafir assured him. "I just want to get our client back to the city where he'll be safe and won't be trespassing on anyone's land."

"All right..." There was a brief pause. "Your client..." A glint of a shotgun barrel flashed in the sun. "The idiot in the shack," came the now-amused throaty voice. "Get him off my land—I'll give you five minutes."

Zafir moved cautiously from behind the bare bush. It had been the snow that clung to its branches that had offered any real cover. He was surprised that the rancher didn't demand Jade's visual, as well. He had to know she was there. He'd already motioned to Jade to move back toward the road.

"Stanley," he called. He walked slowly as he headed to the shanty. His hands were in the air. There was a glint to his right as the rancher's shotgun winked in the sunlight.

The rancher was standing in full view with his shotgun trained on him, but with the sun at his back and in Zafir's face, he could make out little. He'd raised his sunglasses to appear less threatening, but that also made him more vulnerable as he couldn't see through the sun's glare. The man could shoot him now and say they'd been trespassing, that he'd been justified. And he was right. They were trespassing.

He approached the shanty slowly, as if it, too, were rigged with an armed attacker rather than just a frightened royal. "Stanley," he said. "Let's get you out of here.

The beaten shanty was only one room, but a closer look told him that it had held up amazingly well through the years. It looked like it was still used. The stone chimney was intact and had soot clinging to it as if someone had recently used it. As he observed that, the broken plank door swung open.

His first look at their client didn't surprise him. He was everything he'd expected and what the photo in his file had portrayed. He was an average-sized man by Moroccan standards. His camera hung around his neck and rested on the top of his belly. His round face was flushed, and his eyes were panicked.

It was always strange, Zafir thought, to see a client for the first time. Who they were on paper was often different from in person. In Stanley's case he was surprised to feel sympathy. He couldn't imagine what this might have been like for him. Hearing gunfire around him, being stuck in a weather-worn, one-room building—having that as his only protection. The man had more than likely never been near firearms, never been this deep into the wilderness. He broke off his thoughts and focused his full attention on getting Stanley the hell out of there.

"I'm Jade's boss," he said, although the truth was that he was Jade's partner, at least in this case. But he guessed that *boss* would have the most clout, get the client out of here without a dispute delaying that. "We're going to get you out of this, Stan," he said. He slipped into the nickname easily. Stan was a man's name; Stanley—somehow that name just grated.

Stanley was shaking slightly. "This is crazy."

"Maybe. But he was justified."

"Justified?"

"You were on his land without permission."

"That's why he was shooting at me?"

"Let's get out of here." He watched behind him to make sure the man was following his instructions. "Follow me. I'll keep you covered."

"He almost killed…" Stanley said as he stopped

as if he couldn't take another step. He looked over his shoulder. "Where's Jade?"

"She'll meet us," Zafir said. "C'mon, keep moving." He doubted the rancher's patience was going to stretch much further. "Follow me. Let's get you out of here." He moved ahead of Stanley until they were past the rancher's position, then he moved behind. That made it difficult for the rancher to get a clear shot of Stanley. While the bulletproof vest wasn't a guarantee of protection, it was more than Stanley had.

"Hurry it up," the rancher bellowed. "I'm not going to shoot you if that's what you're afraid of. Unless, of course, you don't get moving faster than you are."

"Let's go, Stan," Zafir said. He looked to his right and could see a flash of movement—Jade. "Walk in front of me and head for the road. I'm right behind you."

He looked over his shoulder. The rancher was still standing, watching them. His shotgun was in both hands but pointed slightly down. In that moment, he realized that the threat was very close to over.

"Keep quiet and keep moving," Zafir said. "We're not out of the woods yet."

"He won't shoot?" Stanley asked.

Zafir prodded him with the palm of his hand. "Hurry up!" he snapped. He wasn't sure how this assignment was going to get better from here. He was scared it might continue to go south. Only a minute into a face-to-face meeting and already he was losing patience.

Ahead he could see the brush where Jade was now concealed. He moved away from her and toward the road, knowing that she'd follow and keep out of sight for as long as possible as she did so. It wasn't anything they'd discussed, just something he knew in his gut. There were moments where he'd just known what she was thinking, where nothing needed to be said. He'd never experienced anything like that before. And it made him uncomfortable, to say the least. But there was something else. She made him feel like no woman ever had. He'd admit that to no one.

He didn't believe in such things—that one could instantly fall for a person. That was hokey garbage. He'd told Emir that many times. But his twin had his own reasons for believing—his fiancée, Kate. Zafir liked playing the field far too much. There were too many fish in the sea to ever settle for one.

He wouldn't be thinking these things if he thought they were still in crisis. But the rancher appeared satisfied, and the drama appeared to be over. This time when he turned around, he saw Jade just behind him. He motioned ahead of him, so that he could stand between her and the last remnants of danger.

He didn't think about what that might mean. It meant nothing. His need to protect her—his fear

for her, placing himself between her and danger—
it was only what a good man did. But thinking that
and believing it were becoming two completely different things.

# Chapter Nine

"What is wrong with you people?" Stanley demanded five minutes later as he hurried to keep up.

Neither Jade nor Zafir slowed their pace despite their client's plea. At this juncture they preferred to get on the other side of the fence, to the road and safety. They'd left the rancher well behind them, and the road was in sight. But until they reached the highway, neither of them would feel comfortable.

"Is this country all like this?" he demanded. "Are you all crazy?"

"This isn't the normal way of things, Stan, but property is a big deal in Wyoming. You can't just step onto someone's land," Zafir said calmly and without slowing his stride. But Stanley was testing his patience in a way no other client ever had. He had to remember, Stanley was Moroccan. He'd never been to the States before. According to the file, he'd never been anywhere. He was in a culture that was unfamiliar to him. "He has rights as a landowner.

You've got to remember that while you're here. Especially if you plan to take pictures in the countryside."

"He could have asked me to leave," Stanley said. "That would have been the civil thing to do. There was no reason to try to kill me."

"He could have killed you, Stan. He didn't."

"He has a point, Zafir," Jade said. "I have to say that threatening to shoot him was a little over the top."

"A little?" Stanley asked, his voice an octave higher than normal. He opened the back door of the Pathfinder. "It was craziness. This wouldn't have happened at home. This…"

"You're wrong there, Stan," Zafir said, thinking of the many cases he'd handled at home, in Morocco. He looked at Jade, and she smiled as if she was completely aware of where his thoughts had gone.

"Don't bolt like that again, Stan. We can't protect you if we don't know where you are."

"You don't know the country…" Jade began.

"You're not kidding," Stanley muttered. "This would never happen in Morocco," he repeated, obviously set in what he believed no matter what Zafir said to the contrary.

"Never." Jade smiled as she looked at Zafir, because they both knew it could happen anywhere and had. She might not have worked a case in Morocco, but she'd certainly read the files. "I believe this is yours." She tossed the lens cap to Stanley who caught it with one hand and put it in his pocket without a word of thanks.

"Another thing, Stan," Zafir said. "You can only take pictures of land where you have permission or on land that's not privately owned."

"You're kidding me," Stanley muttered.

Zafir was turning onto the highway before anyone spoke again.

"Is there something you're not telling us, Stanley?" Jade asked. "The rancher's aggression is extreme, depending how you view such things, but explainable. But what happened earlier, the shooting at the apartment, that's not. Is there a reason that someone would want to shoot you?"

"No," he said almost too sharply, too abruptly. "I don't want to think about that."

"That won't make it go away," Jade said.

"Why do you think I left? I couldn't deal. No one has ever shot at me. And now it's happened twice. This is craziness. You should report that man. The rancher, I mean. I bet we could look up…"

"You were at fault, Stan," Zafir interrupted him.

"From what you've said, Stanley, this incident aside, whoever was shooting at you in Jackson has no motive that we know of. Is that what you're saying?"

Zafir hoped the tact Jade was taking, of feigning ignorance of the inheritance, might lead Stan to reveal anything he knew.

"I'm not important enough for someone to want to kill." Stanley's voice began to shake.

"What do you have that someone else wants?"

"Nothing!"

Zafir looked in the rearview mirror and saw that Stanley was looking out the window; his lips were tight and one hand clutched the door handle as if he were prepared to flee. Again.

"It's all been crazy," he muttered. But his left hand was clenched in a fist and he was chewing his bottom lip.

Zafir was certain that he knew something about the earlier attack. Maybe he knew who or why—possibly both. Somehow they were going to have to get him to trust them enough to tell them. It was only then that they'd be able to protect him.

"I thought this was the countryside. You know, untouched—safe, full of friendly farmer types." Stanley scowled. "Bucolic, like Heidi land."

"Heidi land," Zafir mouthed the words, an amused smile on his face.

"It was misrepresented. Nothing like the brochure said it was," Stanley said.

"You can't just appear on someone's land and expect to be welcomed," Jade said.

"So I'm learning," Stanley said rather sardonically and nodded. "The locals aren't friendly at all." He paused for breath, looking out the window with a grim expression. "He would have killed me."

Zafir met Jade's look. They both knew that Stanley was overwhelmed by the back-to-back experiences with firearms. It was a logical assumption. What layman wouldn't be if faced with the same situation?

For a minute there was silence.

"Insanity," Stanley muttered. He was stuck in a track he just couldn't seem to clear.

"You might be right, Stan, but right doesn't make you safe. We do. So in the future, I don't care what you think," Zafir said. "As long as we're protecting you, when we give an order we need you to follow it. No more taking off."

"Orders?"

Zafir glanced in the rearview mirror. The tone of their client's voice had changed. His eyes had narrowed and his nostrils flared. He'd just acquired major attitude. In fact, Stanley was now sitting up straight and there was a look about him that was very clearly royal. The look in his eyes was unleashed outrage, like they were minions who had failed him. "There weren't any orders, and even if there were, I'm..."

"Suggestions, Stanley," Jade said, cutting him off.

Zafir's mouth quirked as he glanced at Jade. She smiled. It seemed their client with the wallflower personality actually had some backbone. Of course, that backbone had almost gotten him killed.

"I hired you, not the other way around," he muttered before slumping back in his seat. "And you people are crazy. I'm not sure I want to listen to any of you."

"I assume you mean the man shooting at you, not us," Zafir said. "You were trespassing. Trespassing is an offense, it means you were on property…"

"I know what it means," he interrupted with an edge to his voice. "I have an excellent command of the English language."

"And yet you failed to read the no trespassing sign?" Jade asked.

"No, I saw it and the no hunting sign," Stanley added. "But I thought as long as I wasn't hunting, it was okay." He took a breath. "Besides, I was clearly unarmed, yet he shot at me anyway. I'm not sure what he thought. He couldn't miss the camera. It was really unforgivable," he said with a hard edge to his voice. He seemed to be determined to ignore everything they had said including what Jade had just told him about taking photos. "He wanted to kill me for stepping on his scrub excuse for a field." His voice rose two octaves, as if that would put emphasis on the outrage he felt.

"It doesn't matter what you think of his property, Stanley." Frustration was clear in Jade's voice.

"So, here's the deal. We're here to protect you. We already know from the attack in Jackson that there's a very real possibility that someone wants you dead,"

Zafir said. "The best way to ensure that happens is to leave our protection. The best way not to…"

"I've got it," Stanley interrupted. "You're right." He ran a hand through his thinning dark curly hair. "But I'm not going back to Jackson." He dropped his hand. "I don't think it's safe. I'd like to go to Casper. I've read good things about it, and there are some good photography spots."

"Agreed," Zafir said.

Stanley had fallen into a plan that was already in the works. Their relocation specialist, Leslie, was at this moment getting that option together. It was the best-case scenario all around. But what Stanley didn't know was that it was also temporary.

"Caspar, Wyoming, it is," Zafir said with a look at Jade. "Do you know what I'm thinking, Stan?" He didn't wait for the man to reply. "I think that there's a little more to this than a photographic vacation."

Jade glanced at him. The real reason that their company was hired had been kept secret from them when Nassar has been contracted. That secret had propelled a gunman to go after Stanley this morning. Stanley wasn't the easy, risk-free tourist he'd been portrayed as—not even close.

"Everything you can tell us will help us do our job." Jade turned to look at him. "Stanley?" she asked softly, ready to use her wiles if that's what it took.

"You have everything you need to know," he said as he looked out the window. His lips were taut and his expression troubled. It was obvious that he had no more to say.

Jade frowned. Obviously her wiles had an expiration date. She looked at Zafir, and when he glanced at her, his dark eyes were filled with amusement. But it was the twitch of his lips and the dimple that she hadn't seen before that almost had her laughing. His humor was contagious. She smiled. If the situation wasn't so troubling she might have outright laughed.

Silence filled the vehicle as the miles disappeared behind them.

A hawk swooped low, its shadow dipping over the highway, paralleling their progress before it swept up and away.

They were alone with one indignant client and more questions than answers.

## Chapter Ten

Stanley fell asleep fifteen minutes into the drive to Casper.

"This hasn't ended. Whoever was after him in Jackson is still on the loose, still after him," Jade said quietly despite the fact that Stanley was out cold.

"At least we were able to get a safe house in Casper arranged. With any luck we can get a quiet night, some rest, and get a plan together before any more trouble hits. In the meantime, we're going to have to lay down the law with Stan," Zafir said.

"Who would try to shoot him?" she mused. "Is it all about this inheritance or is there something else?"

Zafir didn't reply. He was concentrating on the road, which was still treacherous.

"You should have let me drive," Jade said with a smile. "I have more experience with winter driving." His driving had been fine, but she'd felt like something needed to be said, something mundane to take their minds out of high gear.

"Are you telling me that I'm driving too slow? First it's too fast, then…" He chuckled. "I think you like to be in control. You don't like being in the passenger seat." He glanced over at her with a half smile. He looked at the speedometer. "All right, you have a point. Once the heat was off and we had Stanley, I slowed down a bit."

"A bit," she said with a laugh.

"Unlike a certain motorcycle rider…" He let the rest trail.

"Look, I'm not usually that risky of a driver." She wasn't sure why she was explaining it to him, but he made her want to justify herself, or maybe the truth was, to prove herself. "It wasn't a normal occurrence—the motorcycle, I mean. I was desperate. Running out of time and…"

"A cab wasn't a consideration," he interrupted with a smile.

"Never," she said with a laugh. "Too far for one."

They smiled at each other. It was a relief to switch the conversation to a lighter topic. It gave them a chance to recharge and open their minds to other possibilities and angles of the case. Angles that they might not have considered in the heat of the back-to-back crises they'd just experienced.

Time passed. It was getting dark. The temperature began to drop as the sun began to slip below the horizon. The highway was rapidly becoming even more slick than it had been before. Now it was a sheet of ice, making driving, even on the interstate, treacherous. With the small city of Casper visible in the distance, Stanley stirred and stretched.

"Casper," Stanley said as he came fully awake and saw the highway sign. "Will it be safe?"

"We'll make it safe," Jade assured him. "I think we've had more than enough excitement for one day."

THEY STOOD OUTSIDE the west unit of a small duplex near the outskirts of Casper. The other unit was empty. The duplex was monitored by a camera that had been placed there during another assignment and kept the perimeter of the building secure.

"We're set up and the area is clear," Jade said to Zafir an hour later. Leslie had let them know that the office was swamped, and although a more permanent place would be found, for now, they weren't at the top of the list. That was one thing that Jade loved about Nassar—none of the brothers who headed the branches of the agency pulled rank unless absolutely necessary. Every employee's area of expertise was respected.

"This case started out as one thing and morphed into another. Everything so far has been out of the norm. I feel like I might have missed something," Jade said with a frown. She folded her arms beneath her breasts, holding back a shiver. The sun had set, and with the wind and the snow cover there was a winter chill to the air despite the fact that it was late April.

"The area's clear. You determined that five minutes before you did the second check." He looked at her, a frown on his face. "Don't question yourself."

She smiled, but the gesture seemed forced; her lips felt stiff.

"You've got it covered," he said with a note of finality.

He was right. The street and the surrounding area were as benign and quiet as it appeared the previous times that she had checked. Other than a sparrow flitting from one bare branch to another, there was nothing except a few parked cars and a shroud of snow.

They'd stopped for takeout on their way into the city. Now it was only a matter of making a plan and getting some rest.

They went up four wooden steps that led to the front door. In the entranceway, there were two doors, an exterior screen and an interior security door with a dead bolt.

"While you were checking the outside perimeter, I hooked Stan up with an online game. Keeps his mind off doing anything stupid like running again, at least in the short term," Zafir said as he closed the doors behind them.

"I think his 'adventure' cured him of that. At least for now."

They entered a small hallway that led to a minuscule storage area to the left and ran eight feet beyond that to open into a one-bedroom suite.

"Brilliant," she said as she glanced over at the couch where Stanley was completely focused on a game.

*"Space Odds?"* she asked, guessing that it would be the game Zafir had mentioned earlier that he had been playing online with Faisal a few days ago. She glanced back at Zafir and then wished she hadn't. His eyes were too hot, dark and intense, and inescapable. She looked away, her gaze shifting around the room. She would have looked at anything but him to regain her equilibrium.

"Intriguing name for a game. I'll have to give it a go one day." She couldn't think of another thing to say. She knew it was a game of many levels that involved taking over interplanetary colonies. She knew, too, that Zafir wasn't much of a gamer. That was Faisal's department. She guessed from that and what had already been said that it was an easy way for the brothers to stay in contact even when separated by cases and continents.

She drifted into the small kitchen that was open to the living area and separated only by a miniscule counter. She was at a loss as to what to do. Earlier, it had been different. There had been danger. Danger had allowed her to go into action with a natural surety and no thought to anything but protecting the client. Now she was facing what she considered a legend in the agency. With nothing to distract her, there was nothing to buffer his proximity. There wasn't an unsub threatening them or even a client needing attention. They were trapped in a shoe box of an apartment, and she was more aware of him than she wanted or needed to be. She couldn't explain the why of it, but he'd always intrigued her in a way his twin, Emir, never had.

She'd admired his skill and had studied him since she'd first signed on with Nassar. She'd followed each of his cases, going through the details to hone her own skills. She'd learned from one of the best, and in the process, she had to admit, she'd become infatuated with the idea of him. But Zafir in a cold two-dimensional file was not the three-dimensional man filling this small space. In person, he was so much more.

"Hey Stanley, made the high score yet?" she asked with absolutely no clue what the high score might be. She'd never played an online game in her life and wasn't sure how Zafir had immediately realized that Stanley had. It definitely wasn't in the file, but there appeared to be a few things that weren't in the file.

"Exceeded it," he said with a quiet smile.

"That's great," she said with little enthusiasm as she glanced around the kitchen area and saw a coffeemaker along with coffee on the counter, a toaster and a microwave. She opened the fridge. Someone had made sure that there was milk, bread, a small jar of jam, and eggs. She closed the door.

An hour passed and Stanley had put the game aside.

He stood up, yawning.

"You can have the bedroom, Stanley," she said. "You must be exhausted."

He smiled at her with a look of irony. "Considering everything," he said. "I am and I'll take it." He glanced at the Murphy bed that hadn't been opened. "The two of you will have to fight for that," he said now looking at the Murphy bed with disdain before he went into the bedroom and closed the door.

"We need a plan," Jade said to Zafir. "Stanley seems to think he'll be safe here for the next ten days while he takes pictures in and around the city." She shrugged, knowing that they were on the same page with this, seeing the truth in his eyes, knowing his words before he spoke. "I didn't tell him that it wasn't a good idea. In fact, I didn't say anything. So he thinks that's what's going to happen. But staying in Casper..."

"Not going to happen," he interrupted.

"We're both agreed on that. Whoever is after Stanley may or may not track us here. We can't take the chance that they do, so there's an expiration date on this location."

It was dark, but neither considered turning on another light. It was as if the soft glow from one small reading lamp was enough, as if anything brighter might prove a distraction. She glanced across the room to the Murphy bed that hadn't been pulled down. She imagined that they would toss a coin to see who would use it, or maybe she would give it to him. Jade doubted she would sleep much at all that night; it was always like that after an adrenaline rush. It took her hours to come down and this time even longer, thanks to the presence of Zafir.

She didn't want to admit how he made her feel, not even to herself. She didn't believe in falling in love at first sight. But having him in the same room, for her to feign any kind of sleep when he was warm and hot and hard…

Holy Hannah, this was ridiculous. She'd never felt like this, and she sure as hell shouldn't feel like this now. Besides, her job was too important. Yet the attraction had been immediate and only fueled by her fascination with him for the last year. Ever since she was hired by Nassar she had followed his cases. She'd been drawn to him and she wasn't sure why except there was something in the way that he presented himself. It was strange to think that of a man she hadn't officially met. But it had started from the first moment she'd seen a picture hanging on the office wall of all the brothers. And it was also in the way Faisal had spoken about him. All of it culminated into that one time that she'd participated in an online video meeting that had brought together staff from both the Wyoming and the Moroccan office. She'd watched his mannerisms, listened to his thoughts and said little in that meeting. She'd been overwhelmed with how being in the same time and space as him, even virtually, had made her feel.

Not that that should be a surprise; hard and fast, it was how she ran her life. Everything turned on a dime, from her assignments to her vacations. She'd been known to organize a trip to South America and been on the plane within the space of forty-eight hours. It was not only how one got the best flight deals—last-minute hands down, every time—it was also more exciting. It was why she did what she did and ran her private life as she had. It was also how one made huge mistakes—her last relationship, for one.

She took a deep breath. That was the biggest lie she had ever told herself. Every one of her past relationships had been a mistake. They'd been based on what her body had told her rather than her head, and they'd all turned out badly. Only trips and assignments such as these seemed to work by turning on a dime. Based on past experience, she needed to ignore how she felt about Zafir. Her position at Nassar could hang in the balance. Getting it on with the man who was, in any other situation, her boss was a bad idea. Getting it on with a man who had a reputation for loving and leaving was not smart. But the voice of reason didn't seem to have any power over the feelings that had sprung to life from the first moment she'd laid eyes on him.

She watched as he moved to the window. He stood there silently looking at the street. His thoughts were as silent as his presence.

In the bedroom, Stanley's snores were rhythmic and so consistent that they were almost background noise. She imagined he was sleeping through the trauma, dream-free. He'd had enough trauma for a lifetime. The poor man had had a rough introduction to the United States of America.

Minutes ticked by. She made a pot of coffee and offered Zafir a cup.

She sat down on the opposite end of the couch from him.

"We can keep him safe here, in the States. Yet the danger looks more pervasive than that. We'll know more, hopefully soon," he said, and took a sip of coffee. "I've never liked the waiting game."

"What about Morocco? Can he be kept safe there?" she asked. It had to be considered. "Eventually, he has to go home."

Jade's phone beeped. She pulled it out and answered. "That was Colette," she said a few minutes later. Colette headed all administrative functions including supervising three other office staff. She was the heart of their office, and nothing happened there without her say so. "There was one Moroccan who cleared customs at JFK the day before Stanley and from there went on to Casper via Salt Lake City and from there on to Jackson." She frowned. "He didn't ring any alarms going through security. The only heads-up anyone had was my query. By then he was already long gone." She paused. "His name is Mohammed Jadid."

"So who is Mohammed Jadid?" Zafir asked.

"As in his relationship to Stanley, or if there is one?" she asked. "They've found nothing yet. But there's someone on it," she said. "In the meantime, Mohammed flew out of Rabat's international airport." Her gaze locked on his, and she knew that they were still on the same page. "How many Moroccans flew out of Rabat to Jackson, Wyoming, in the last few days? Two," she said, answering her own question.

"It's still a shaky theory," Zafir said.

"True. But it gets more interesting. After Jackson there's no paper trail on this guy. No vehicles rented, no hotel rooms, nothing."

Zafir looked thoughtful. "It is suspicious. The key question would be what's his relationship to Stan, if there is one?"

"That's what we don't know. Maybe there's nothing, but it's not like Moroccan tourists have been beating a path to Jackson in what is normally off season for skiers. Unless, like Stanley, they're into photographing wildlife. This snow was unexpected and won't stay on the ground long."

"So he leaves no trail. But arrives in Jackson and drops immediately out of sight."

"Does he know Stanley or…"

"Is he a hit man hired to take Stan out?"

She bit her lip.

"Worst-case scenario," Zafir said darkly.

"And Stanley doesn't stand a chance," Jade finished.

"The odds that he's not our sniper aren't great."

"The office is on it. I don't know how soon we'll get anything."

She went to the window as if there were answers there.

"I've been in contact with Emir. He's going to see about getting the contract extended past the original ten days." He looked tired. "If it comes to that…"

They both knew that they'd do what they had to do to successfully close this case and return the client safely to Morocco. Whether they had to escort him or not, they'd get him there. But for now that wasn't an issue. For now, the issue was keeping him alive, and to do that they needed to pin down the threat against him.

"There's something we can't put our finger on. I know you sense it, too. Like Stanley's…"

"Keeping secrets. Knows more than he's telling," he said. "That's a given. We both know that. I think we need to have a long talk with the man."

Another snore rocked the room, and despite the

new twist in the case or maybe because of that, they smiled at each other. Stanley was like no other client. It was becoming a very quirky case.

"He's a challenge," she said, but her smile slipped as she met Zafir's eyes, which seemed to smoke with passion. It was a strange state of affairs. She hadn't been with him long enough to know him. Yet she knew him like she didn't know many people in her life. And that frightened her for it could change everything because she'd never wanted a man more.

## Chapter Eleven

"He's not giving us anything," Jade whispered, and they both knew that she referred to Stanley. "At least not voluntarily."

It was still dark as they headed into the early hours of the second day that they'd been on this case. It looked like they'd be staying in Casper rather than moving on. The Wyoming office was stretched thin, as a family emergency had one of their office staff on leave and the others even more overwhelmed with priority demands. As there was no sign that their accommodations had been jeopardized, they prioritized the needs of yet another case over immediately finding a safe house for them. They were uncomfortably crowded but safe. It could be another day before they would move again. In the meantime, they would wait it out.

The streetlamp glinted, sending tendrils of light across the short expanse of counter and providing a muted glow in the kitchen. The rest of the small area remained dark. She flicked on the table light beside the sofa and sat down just to rest for a minute.

She must have fallen asleep, because the next thing she heard was her text alert. She looked at her phone. She'd been sleeping for two hours. The message was from Colette in the Jackson office warning her that she'd be phoning in the next minute.

Zafir stood by the sink looking out the window, as if he could see into the night.

He turned around.

"You're awake," he said.

"Stanley?" she asked.

"Sleeping."

Her phone rang and she answered. A few minutes later she disconnected.

"We've got our answer about our second Moroccan," she said to Zafir.

"Who is he?"

"Mohammed Jadid is Stanley's first cousin. They're relatively close in age."

"Let me guess, he stands to inherit should something happen to Stanley," Zafir said.

"Actually, that's the strange thing. No. He's a cousin on the maternal side, while Stanley's uncle is his father's brother. All inheritance goes through the paternal side. This cousin is out of the loop as he's related on the wrong side to have a chance at the inheritance."

"Yet he arrived in Wyoming, we assume, following Stan. Interesting. I don't know what to think."

"I think we need to ask Stanley," she said as she got up and moved to the small kitchen area that openly adjoined the other living area.

"You're right, but timing is everything. We both know that it won't take much to have him heading home. He's on edge and depending on what the deal is with this cousin…"

"Agreed. I'll try to gently lead him." She threaded her fingers through her hair and then dropped her hands to the counter. "There's something else. I'd forgotten. You know when we were in Jackson? It was right after we arrived. I was just playing at getting to know him. You know, asking superficial questions."

"Before the code changed?"

"Exactly. I don't know if it's important or not but…" She shook her head. "No, that's wrong. It could be very important…"

It had been forgotten in the rumble of all that had happened. Yesterday had gone by in a blur as they'd secured the unit and made Stanley comfortable.

"What?" Zafir cut her off as he came over and sat down on a small straight-backed in the living area only a few feet from the kitchen counter where she stood.

"Stanley told me that he got his nickname from his brother."

"Brother? That wasn't in the file. I assumed he was an only child."

"The file didn't speak to the issue one way or the other."

"Prince Rashad would have known," he said. "He obviously didn't think it was important."

"Maybe it isn't." She shrugged. "But we have to cover all angles."

"The case began low-key. The file wasn't detailed as a result," he said thoughtfully. He looked at her, waiting for her to fill him in.

"According to Stanley, his brother has been dead for years. He was older than Stanley. His brother gave him the nickname based on a cartoon character. Apparently his brother told him he looked like the character called Stanley and he's been called that ever since."

"And as a grown man continues to go by that name," Zafir said. "Interesting. So is the information on the brother. What was the cause of death?"

"I don't know. Stanley only said it was an accident," she said, knowing that cause of death could reveal more things sometimes than a living being ever could. "He died twenty-five years ago, according to Stanley. So, since Stanley's thirty-nine now, he was only a child when his brother died." She shrugged. "There was no time to ask more questions. We were shot at not long after the subject came up."

"Considering how this case has changed, we need

to find out how his brother died—his parents, too. Although their deaths were a few years later. At least that part was in the file." He glanced over at the bedroom. "Let's not mention any of this to Stan. For now, we'll get the official record. Later, we'll get the unofficial report from Stan. Like I said before, I think if we push him now we chance frightening him, having him insisting on going back to Morocco. I'd like to have a clearer understanding of the threat before that happens."

"I'll contact the office," Jade said. "I have his parents' given names and approximate ages. I was hoping to confirm the information the file has."

"Good plan," he agreed. "Let's make sure that what is there is accurate."

Silence drifted between them and she pulled out her phone and began an internet search. She was looking for information on Stanley's brother. But other than a dry layout of lineage to the Moroccan throne, there was no mention of a sibling.

"I just did an online search while I was sitting here. Nothing." She frowned as she looked up at him, her fingers poised as if contemplating entering another search. "Interesting. So, we don't have much on his brother, not even a given name."

She frowned. They'd hoped that while they lay low, Stanley would feel safe and tell them what he knew. Interrogation, they feared, would cause him to withdraw. But giving him rope hadn't given them any more information, either.

Early-morning light drifted into the room. It reminded them that they were quickly losing the luxury of time.

"I'll make coffee," Zafir said.

"Great," she said, and returned his smile with a look of appreciation as she picked up her phone, texting her request to Colette in the main office.

"Colette," she said to Zafir five minutes later, "wanted you to know that the new admin is working out splendidly. I believe those were her exact words. We were afraid that training would complicate the shortage of support staff but it looks like she's going to help not hinder."

"She moved faster than I expected on hiring help. In fact, I didn't know the new hire was already in the office being trained." He shrugged. "Bonus, she's a quick learner and should take the edge off our shortage of staff."

"That's not all Colette's done since we last spoke. She's followed up on our case, as well. She checked with Moroccan authorities. They couldn't find confirmation of Stanley's brother's death, either. They found his birth records and we have a name, Chasi el Eloua, and a year of birth but nothing else. He's eight years older than Stanley. It's interesting that the mother's death record is registered twenty-two years ago and his father's twenty years ago. They both died of natural causes. That is if you call dying before you hit sixty natural." She sighed. "I know it's off topic, but that frightens me."

"What?"

"Dying in a hospital of sickness—heart disease, cancer or… I'd rather die in the field with my boots on." She shook her head as if dispersing the morose thoughts.

"Wouldn't we all?" he said with an easy smile, and switched the topic back to the case. "So, his brother was dead before his parents died. That leaves Stan the sole survivor and beneficiary of his parents' life insurance."

"Exactly. That's what he's been living on. But, there's more."

He waited expectantly.

"So far everything is adding up just as it should. Except…" She paused. "We're really stumbling on confirming Chasi el Eloua's death." She took a cup of black coffee from Zafir. "Thanks." She wasn't sure when he'd learned how she drank her coffee. Personal preferences seemed to blur into the background of the case.

"Depending what year he died, the record might not be online."

"Colette checked that. The year Stanley claims Chasi died, records were entered into a manual system that was transferred later to computer. Usually that's just straight data entry. It could have been as simple a mistake as the data entry clerk turned two pages instead of one. That was our initial thought. But we've just discovered that wasn't the case. There is no paper record, either." She ran a hand through her hair. "But I know what you mean. He died in an institution, mistakes, papers not being filed—rare, but it happens."

"Exactly," he agreed. "Twenty-five years ago when Chasi supposedly died, the internet was in its infancy. It may take a bit more digging." He pulled out his phone. "I'll get Tara on it. Colette has enough to do with training and dealing with what we've got going on already."

"I might have a suspicious mind, but in the meantime let's just keep this search as well between the two of us." She looked up and gave a rather forced smile at the sight of Stanley standing tentatively in the bedroom doorway. Her mind went back over what she had said, and she hoped that he hadn't heard their whispered conversation.

"I can't sleep. I'll try to nap later," he said as if his sleep patterns were on everyone's mind.

He hadn't dressed and seemed unfocused in his saggy white boxers and a ratty T-shirt. The minimal dress showed off a bit of a belly and hairy legs.

"Get dressed, man," Zafir growled. "There's a lady present."

"I'm sorry." He looked slightly befuddled. "I'm not used to having company. I usually— I live alone…" He stammered as if that explained every-thing. His voice trailed off as his face reddened and he turned away, heading back into the bedroom.

"I think the stress of it all, being cooped up with us for so long, is getting to him." She stood up and carried the coffee cups to the sink. When she turned around, Zafir was on his phone.

"The van hasn't been moved yet," Zafir said after he ended the call.

"You're kidding me. I didn't give it a thought… just assumed." She clenched her fist. Mistake.

"I just spoke to Destiny," he said, referring to an-other of their office staff. "She says the app is still ac-tive and the rental claims they've been overwhelmed and understaffed."

"Sounds familiar," Jade said with a laugh.

"I'm going back. See if I can find anything we might have missed." Zafir offered one of his rare smiles and revealed a second dimple that she hadn't known existed. "I should have gone back yesterday."

"It was dark by the time we set up here," she re-minded him.

"True, but that's never stopped…"

"A Nassar agent," she interrupted him with a smile. "Nothing you can do about it now. But speak-ing of yesterday, Stanley said something last night. He said there was something odd about the steering right from the outset. I thought nothing of it with the weather conditions as they were. I thought…"

"Inexperienced winter-condition driver," Zafir finished.

"Exactly."

There was silence as they both contemplated what that might mean.

"Did Stanley end up in the ditch because of poor driving or…"

"You're saying that someone knew that I would rent it, that I was picking him up." She frowned. "So did they want to hurt me or Stanley?"

"Maybe neither. Maybe it's a crazy theory." His fingers trailed over his chin, and for a moment he ran a thumb and forefinger on either side before dropping his hand. "Why did they rent you something like that, a vehicle that I would almost say was too old to be rented out?" His eyes met hers, probing, seeking answers. "Were there other vehicles available?"

"Of course there were but none of them were appropriate. I wanted something that could hold all his luggage and…" She paused. "I wanted an SUV." She considered the possibilities. "Actually, there was an SUV on the lot. They said it was rented. I never thought about it. I was running late." She pulled her hair back and away from her face. "You're suggesting that there was something wrong with the van? That they wanted me to take it knowing it would break down?"

"Possibly?" Zafir rubbed a hand along the dark shadow on his chin. "I'm no mechanic. But I'm thinking more along the line of other clues. Something we might have missed. We didn't go over the van that closely. Destiny is checking into who rented that last SUV."

"We didn't think there was…"

"Tampering? It's probably a long shot but something we shouldn't discount."

"I didn't think of that… I should have thought of some of this right at the time of rental."

"There was no need to think about it at the time," Zafir said. "It was a simple case then. If I remember right, I told you to take a good book."

"You did," she said with a slight smile, grateful for his attempt at humor.

"I've got a text and a name," he said as he looked at his phone. "The SUV was rented to a group of college students. They took it up to the resort."

"No threat."

"Exactly," he agreed.

"Look, I'll go back. You stay here with Stan. You're better with him," he said before she could protest. "Shock him a little. Push him like we haven't done yet."

"You mean tell him about Morocco? Is that wise?"

"Yes. But don't tell him about the will. See what he knows, what he might volunteer himself."

"When he hears, he may want to go back, or worse, run again."

"He might," Zafir replied. "But I doubt if he'll get by you twice."

Jade could feel color rise in her cheeks at the compliment. But another thought had her more concerned. "I don't know if I can stop him if he decides he's going back."

"Let's do everything in our power to make sure that doesn't happen."

UNLIKE HIS COUSIN STANLEY, Mohammed would never be a prince and it was all because of his parents, but he blamed his mother most. The stupid hag had birthed him and left him and the latter was the only good thing she'd ever done. He'd been screwed from the beginning. The royal lineage came down through the paternal side and was how Stanley became part of the in crowd and why he, Mohammed, did not. As a result, he despised his entire family. He was only the cousin of a minor prince, nothing more, and that had reflected negatively on him his entire life, or at least that was how he felt. Taking Stanley out would be easy; he'd anticipated he'd have it wrapped up in a matter of days.

But Stanley had surprised him. He hadn't expected him to have protection—someone who would shoot back. It wouldn't happen again. Trust Stanley to get a woman to defend him. He would take her out as easily as he'd take Stanley out. She'd only won the first round because of the element of surprise.

*Stanley.*

The name sent an unpleasant shiver that snaked through him like a bitter tonic. He'd had no use for him as a child, and he doubted he'd become any more impressive since. He hadn't seen him in a long time, and it was only when he'd been approached about this job that he had realized there was even a problem. He couldn't say no. The reward was too high. But it was strange. The whole thing had made him uneasy, brought back childhood memories that he'd thought were long forgotten. He'd never liked Stanley. He'd liked Stanley's crazy brother much better even though he had frightened him. Despite that, he felt no regret about saying yes to taking out Whining Stanley. There'd been better names for him, taunts that had him in tears.

It had all been so easy.

In the beginning.

Now it had all fallen apart.

"Where the hell has he gone?" he snarled through gritted teeth. His heart pounded with the thought that he'd lost his prey, that he was gone, swallowed up in the vastness of the United States. He needed to get home. He hated it here. But first he needed to kill Stanley and collect what was owed him.

Time was running out.

Already his contractor was placing unrealistic expectations on him. Unless something changed, he had forty-eight hours to get the job done. After that, either he delivered evidence of success, or it was not just Stanley who would be on the run.

He looked at the rental agency's locating app. He'd finally been able to hack it and at least now he knew where to start. He could see exactly where the vehicle was. The question remained whether Stanley was with it or not. Anything could have happened, and he wasn't privy to any of that information. What disturbed him was that the vehicle wasn't moving. After being attacked, surely the woman would have advised that taking photographs in the wilderness was a bad idea. So if they weren't taking photographs, what was Stanley doing?

Thirty minutes later he was standing by the white rental van. The sun was just coming up. He turned his flashlight on. The footprints around the van looked like they belonged to at least three people. That was a surprise. Was Stanley traveling with more than just the woman? And if so, who? But the footprints were a confused muddle in the snow, blurring over one another. They were unclear, and even if they weren't, they wouldn't be much help. He was no tracker. It didn't matter; he'd take out whoever was necessary to get to Stanley.

He opened the van door and saw the tourism magazine. He picked it up and flipped the pages. Two pages turned together, one stuck to the other by some type of sticky residue. He pulled the two pages apart and they opened to an overview of the city of Casper,

Wyoming, and beside the page title there was a small black mark made by a pen. It was clearly marked for a reason, as if Stanley had decided that was where he would go next. It made sense. There was an airport there. It would be what he would do if he were Stanley—frightened and alone. Have an escape hatch ready to fly home at a moment's notice. If he hadn't gotten away from him already, he'd make darn good and sure that he wouldn't fly home—not unless he was going there in a body bag. His heart sang at the thought of that. Stanley dead meant that he would have succeeded.

His whole body seemed to relax now that failure didn't seem so imminent. Now he had a place. But there were almost sixty thousand people in Casper and no firm evidence that Stanley was there, too. Small by city standards, but a lot of ground to cover to find one man who may or may not be there. That wouldn't stop him. Especially with this much money on the line. Someone knew something, and they would talk.

"Bingo," he said with not even an inflection of a smile. He had to believe that's where he was. He had no other clues. He dug through his pockets and hauled out a half-smoked cigarette and a pack of matches. He lit the cigarette and tossed the match onto the seat, not caring if it burned or snuffed out. He stepped out and slammed the van door, taking pleasure in imagining that that was the gunshot that left the fatal wound in Stanley's head.

"Bang," he said with a laugh. "You're dead."

## Chapter Twelve

It was past noon when Zafir made a U-turn and pulled in beside the white van that listed in the ditch exactly where they'd left it. Snow still coated the van's windshield and piled two inches high on the roof. He got out of the Pathfinder and walked over to the ditch. He stopped ten feet behind the van. There he crouched down for a better look at the footprints leading up to the van. There were so many, more than just what the three of them had left behind. But it was hard to tell, because they were inlaid in the snow over and around one another, becoming almost a collage of prints.

It hadn't snowed since just before they'd found Stanley yesterday although the weather forecast had threatened more snowfall. He moved closer to the van, bent down and saw what he assumed from the size and depth was a man's print. He lifted his foot, looked at the sole of his shoe and identified the print as his. Then there was a larger print, a sneaker print,

Stan's; and a woman's, smaller, lighter—Jade. But there was another set of prints, ones that didn't match the other three. They were lost at points in the jumble of other prints, but the fourth set never seemed to stray farther than the perimeter of the van. They weren't clear, but what was clear was that someone else had been here. It could have been the rancher, but there were no footprints leading across the field from where the rancher had shot at them. It was possible that he'd come in by road and pulled over, coming to look at the van. That was likely, but his gut was telling him that that wasn't what happened.

There was another option. Actually, he thought as he ran through the possibilities, there were several of them. Whoever was here could be a random stranger. He didn't think that was the best theory. The odds of someone stopping because of an abandoned vehicle, unless they were law enforcement, was slim. Police would have had the van towed. The fact that it was still here made that unlikely.

But there was a third option that troubled him more than any of the others. It all led back to that earlier attack on Jade and Stanley. The person who had shot at them had never been identified as male or female, as American or foreign, and they were now missing. They'd assumed that it could be Stanley's cousin, the Moroccan who had arrived at the Jackson airport and then vanished. But there was no motivation. There were only questions. Why had he arrived and disappeared? Who was Mohammed hiding from? But those questions only led to others.

Who had followed them here? Had the unsub been able to track the van hours later in the same manner they had—through the rental locating device? The answer was yes—the information was there for anyone who was a capable hacker.

He looked beyond the van and could see Ski-Doo tracks. He assumed that was the rancher checking out the situation. That also explained another set of boot prints, smaller than the other's but bigger than Jade's.

He went over to the van and opened the driver's side door.

His phone rang. He looked at the number and frowned. It was Jake. What was the sheriff of Jackson calling him for?

"Yeah, Jake," he answered.

"Zafir. Look, I know that you're mid-case but I thought you might want to know this. Don't know if it has any connection, but we had a car theft late yesterday afternoon. A silver compact," he said, and then went on to give make and year details. "May be your guy, may not, but suffice it to say he was heading in your direction. At least that's what the witness had to say."

"You don't get many thefts…"

"Exactly," Jake cut him off. "My reason for calling you. A shooting and a car theft in that short a time frame. I'd say there's a good chance that they're connected. But unfortunately, the car theft is out of my jurisdiction now."

"Unfortunately," Zafir said with a hint of irony in his voice. He thought of the Jackson sheriff's lethargy and willingness to not get too worked up about most of the minor crimes that happened within city boundaries. The sheriff's response could have been easily predicted. "Any chance I could…"

"Speak to the witness," Jake finished. "Not a chance. He's already heading home to L.A."

Zafir clenched his fist. He'd expected as much of Jake but still… "Did he get a good description?"

"Nothing much we can go on," Jake said. "Thirties, male and tanned with dark hair. Foreign, too, I believe he said."

Moroccan, possibly, Zafir thought considering the way that things were going.

"This changes things," he muttered to himself as he pocketed his phone. His theory about what may or may not have happened at the rental agency was beginning to fall apart. Unless there was more than one unsub, but there was no evidence supporting that theory.

He looked once again into the van. He leaned far in and saw the brochure still lying on the front seat, but this time it was turned to information on Casper, Wyoming. The pages hadn't been turned there before. Jade had closed the magazine when they'd left. He'd watched her do it.

"Damn," he muttered through clenched teeth. Beside the brochure there was something else, a match. He picked it up. The end was charred. He spun it thoughtfully around between his fingers. Stan didn't smoke.

Someone else had been here. He looked long and hard into the distance. He could see the little shanty. There was nothing else. No sign of the rancher, no sign of movement of any kind. He pulled out his binoculars. He rolled his finger along the adjustment knob, focusing on the little building. There was nothing except a lone deer grazing nearby.

He had suspicions and needed answers. He glanced to his left and beyond the shanty. He'd seen a glimpse of it earlier, a rough country road that more than likely led to the rancher's home.

He strode back to the Pathfinder and put it into gear.

It was time to get those answers.

ZAFIR HAD BEEN gone over three hours, and it felt like six. There was little to watch on television. Earlier there had been no news coverage of what had happened in Jackson and now, all these hours later, it was old news. There was nothing to read and no one to talk to. She hated these kinds of lulls. She shut off the television after only a few minutes, not interested in hearing any of it.

She doubted that Zafir would find anything.

What they had discussed earlier were possibilities, no more. She also knew that he would be in communication only if there was an emergent need. Communications could be intercepted. While there was no identified danger of that, they didn't plan to risk it. Chances were that she would not know anything until he returned sometime later this afternoon or early this evening.

They were still waiting for another safe house. Right now, the only thing that she knew for certain was that the new safe house wouldn't be in either Casper or Jackson, but it would be in Wyoming.

Her phone buzzed, and she took the call from their Marrakech office. When she disconnected, she was more confused than ever. There was a record of Stanley's brother's time at an institution and a notation that he had died. The death had supposedly occurred in a psychiatric hospital in Marrakech twenty-five years ago. He'd committed suicide, according to one of their senior employees. The administrator stated that all they had was the chart information in a hospital file. But there was no copy of a signed record of death. It was all incredibly puzzling. It might mean nothing at all, but it could mean everything.

She turned as she heard Stanley come out of the bedroom. He'd lain down for a nap a few hours after Zafir left. She imagined that the trauma and jet lag combined were doing him in. Few people were prepared for that kind of adrenaline rush. She imagined it would tire most people, but then neither she nor Zafir was "most people." They lived for that rush.

"Coffee?" she asked.

"Please," he replied. "Sugar. One heaping."

She poured him a cup from the pot she'd made only a few minutes ago. She put in the heaping teaspoon of sugar, dropping a spoon into the unstirred mix.

She carried the coffee over to where he was sitting on the couch. He took it in both hands with a smile and a nod.

"There's something I need to tell you," she began.

Stanley's full lips thinned and his dark eyes looked troubled, frightened even as if he were already anticipating the worst. Cynically, she thought he should be afraid because since the attack in Jackson, they'd allowed him to coast. Admittedly he'd suffered traumas the likes of which most civilians were never asked to go through. Still, they'd given him time. They'd given him an evening to think, a night to sleep and recoup. It was more than time to push Stanley.

"My uncle's okay?" he asked when she'd finished the short version of the explosion on his uncle's estate.

She nodded.

"No one died?" He put the coffee down unstirred.

"Your uncle's fine," she repeated.

Relief seemed to push Stanley back against the

couch. He eased his death grip on his coffee cup, but he still looked at her with worry.

"You're close to your Uncle Khaled?"

He nodded and took a sip of coffee.

"Why don't we know about him?" she asked softly. "Why wasn't your relationship in the file?"

"There was no need…" His frown deepened.

"You lived with him for a few years after your father died."

"So?"

"Why didn't you at least tell us?"

"It had no relevance and it was a long time ago. I mean, he's my uncle and we're in contact, but when I lived with him I wasn't twenty yet."

She walked a short distance away before turning to face him. It was a tactic that she'd used before when a client had been unwilling to reveal information. Not asking the most relevant questions first to put them slightly off guard.

"He's your father's brother?" She'd posed the question that way because she wanted as much as possible for the information to come from Stanley. Maybe then he'd learn to trust her just a bit more.

"Yes." He folded his arms. "Where are you going with this?"

"The authorities are fairly certain that the explosion wasn't an accident."

Stanley sank into the couch as if he wanted to disappear. Then he straightened up and leaned forward.

The eyes that met hers would have been steely determination in another man, but somehow it was hard to attribute that trait to Stanley. "Was anyone hurt?"

"A gardening assistant was killed," Jade said. "That's not public news."

"What do you mean?"

"Just that the authorities are still investigating." Darn, she thought, she shouldn't have said as much as she had. Stanley didn't need to know that the outcome from the explosion had been kept under wraps.

Silence sifted through the room. Stanley seemed immersed in his own thoughts. Minutes passed. Finally, he leaned forward and looked at her with new determination on his face. "I've got to go back. Make sure my uncle is taken care of. He's not young. He…" He stopped, his lips were pressed tightly together, and his face was flushed.

There was no doubt in his voice, no compromise, and Jade felt her stomach sink. She'd never met this side of Stanley, and she only hoped that it was controllable. The last thing they needed to do now was to go back to Morocco, to the heart of danger. It was why she'd held back on the questions and on what she told him for as long as she had.

"Aren't there other relatives your uncle is close to?" Jade asked. "One of your cousins, perhaps. They could check on him."

He skated right over that suggestion, his breathing coming fast, almost panicked. "My uncle. He needs my help. I should never have left. Not only that, but the rescue…" His voice trailed off.

"Rescue?"

"I work with a local dog rescue. I organized more than one fund-raiser for them," he said. "I had three fosters before I left. They've been adopted since," he said with quiet pride. "The rescue pays me a small salary. I bring in for them twice that through promotions. That's the deal. I wish it could be more. That I could take less from them, but until now I had no other income."

"What do you mean until now?"

"Nothing. I…I had life insurance from my parents but there was no adjustment for inflation." He shrugged rather pathetically. "In today's world, it's not enough to live on."

She didn't push the point. She was too surprised at this side of him, a charitable Stanley, passionate, if his voice was any indication, about a cause.

She changed the subject. It was something to remember for the future, but nothing she needed now. They had more important, immediate considerations. "Do you know any reason someone would have wanted to kill…"

"Was it the old stone cottage on the southeast corner?" Stanley interrupted in a slightly shaky voice.

"It was. What do you know about it, Stanley?"

"My uncle loved to read there in the afternoon."

"So there was a good chance he should have been

there that afternoon?" A thought came to her. "What about you, Stanley? Have you ever been in that cottage?"

"A few times."

The way he said it, the way his eyes didn't meet hers, if she were to guess, she would say he was underplaying his answer.

"Were they trying to kill my uncle?"

"I don't know, Stanley. Do you know anything about his finances?"

"What are you implying?" Stanley asked, with outrage tingeing his words and a flush to his pale face. "Are you saying that I helped him for his money?" He took an outraged breath. "That wasn't the case. I wasn't there for his money." He repeated. "I wasn't."

It was becoming clear that whatever allowance his uncle had made for his death, Stanley knew nothing about it.

"Money changes a lot of things, Stanley." She wasn't quite ready to give up.

"I'm not his beneficiary. He would have told me if I were. Uncle is too organized and efficient to keep anything like that secret, so don't even imply it."

"I didn't imply anything."

"You had that look, Jade," he said. "We might not have known each other long, but sometimes what you think reads on your face."

She took a mental step back. She hadn't expected

that, because she'd made a conscious effort to appear as bland-faced as possible.

He shook his head. "But you're right."

"About what, Stanley?"

"Money—not the will. Seriously, I don't know anything about one. I do know he'd talked about leaving his money to charity." He shook his head and his lips were pressed together even tighter than they had been before, as if something else was bothering him. "But we did have an agreement. It was between the two of us. Uncle needs help." His voice was muted as if they were not alone in the room. "A trust—a living wage that would begin when I return. In exchange for taking care of him. He had it drawn up just before I left."

"You should have told us that, Stanley—about the trust. It makes it fairly difficult to protect you when we don't have all the facts."

"It wasn't relevant." Color flared in his cheeks; contrary to what she knew of him, his passiveness, his fists knotted as if he wanted to hit something or someone. "I need to go back." He stood up, striding across the short space to the window over the sink. There was purpose and, for the first time, arrogance to his walk. He stood there for a moment before turning to face her. "There's no choice. I can't stay here." His right fist remained clenched. "Book me a flight, immediately."

"Stanley…"

"If you don't—" he cut her off "—then I will."

"No," Jade said, standing up.

"This isn't working."

"We'll make it work, Stanley. But it takes some give on both sides." She moved over to where he was sitting. "It would be a mistake to go now."

"A mistake?" He looked at her with troubled eyes.

"Wait. Give it some time."

"Time?"

"We need to talk about this. Come up with a plan," she said in a gentler tone. She put a hand on his shoulder, hoping to calm him. She knew that she had to change her approach, curb her impatience and her need to ask him the questions that were nagging at her. Instead she swallowed all that back. As she and Zafir had agreed, pushing him too soon could have exactly the opposite effect. He would only become more determined to do what they didn't want him to do right now—return home.

"Are you even sure my uncle is under protection?"

"Yes. It was verified by our Marrakech office. He's in good hands, Stanley."

"You're sure?"

"I'm sure," she replied. "I'm also sure that there's nothing you could do besides endanger yourself if you left right now. Don't forget that you're still a target. Someone has shot at you here. Tried to kill you. Do you want to lead that danger to your uncle?"

His cheeks paled, and she was glad that he'd sat down.

"Without knowing who they are or who else is involved, we would be flying into the unknown and potentially place you in even greater danger than you were in Jackson. And," she drew out the last bit, hoping to give it emphasis, "you could endanger your uncle."

"Uncle isn't as strong as he used to be. This kind of stress…" He broke off, his voice shaky, his face red. "I know what you said, the danger…all of that. I get it."

He stood up and then sat back down as if his legs wouldn't hold him.

"But the truth is that I can't stay here for the amount of time I planned. I can hold off a day, even two, but eventually I'm going home." He gazed at her with a dark look in his eyes. "With or without you. I've got responsibilities." He shook his head. "It was wrong of me to leave. I don't know what I was thinking. I should have known."

She thought of what she knew, of his cousin. Of the law of averages that said the probability of both Stanley and his cousin being here at the same time for different purposes unrelated to each other was highly improbable. It wasn't even a coincidence.

"Let us get you to a safe place, identify who is after you. Contain that threat. Then we'll escort you home."

He didn't disagree.

"That's a promise."

She knew what a weight it could be to worry about an elder. She had seen her mother care for her failing grandmother when she'd been a preteen. With only one parent, she worried about that sometimes. Worried about her mother's old age. For now, that concern was eased by the fact that her mother was a vibrant middle-aged woman living her own life, and should it come to that, she had siblings to fill in any gaps.

The thoughts changed her perception of his situation. She looked at Stanley with new respect.

"I feel better knowing that," Stanley said. His eyes met hers, and she could see the worry in them. "I know that he's under protection, but I want to be there for him."

"He has protection 24/7, and if necessary he'll be removed to a safe house." She put a hand on Stanley's shoulder. "He'll be fine. Now all you need to do is stay with us and keep safe so that eventually you can be there for your uncle. Promise me."

They talked for another ten minutes, and it was only after that that she was able to nudge a reluctant agreement out of him.

She hoped that the handshake held meaning for Stanley, that he was a man of his word. For right now it was only the strength of a handshake that was holding him to a rather shaky promise.

## Chapter Thirteen

Zafir got out of the Pathfinder and walked up the road past the no-trespassing sign. The air was crisp, the wind had wound down, and everything appeared still. Yet he knew that he was being watched. He could sense it in a way that could not be disputed. It just was.

"Hello," he shouted. "Anyone here?" His words echoed across the snow-covered silence.

He walked another ten feet. "Nassar Security," he shouted as if the owner of this isolated piece of land would know who or what that meant. But at least they might know that he was no threat, willing to cooperate.

Nothing.

He walked, pacing himself. He looked from right to left as he checked for danger. It had felt silly to shout who he was when it was clear that no one was here. But his gut told him that wasn't true. Someone was here.

Everything was still. As before, the prairie grass was covered with a layer of snow, brown stalks peeking through and awaiting the greening brush of spring. Somewhere in the midst of all this he knew the owner patrolled. It was just a matter of where. Would he have a sixth sense and know someone had breached his land? Would he be on a distant acre unaware? He kept walking.

"I have a few questions." His words echoed and fell unanswered. He felt rather silly, but he wasn't deterred. "Hello!" Something seemed to move to his right. He wasn't sure if it was real or his imagination. Again, he identified himself with the hope that the words of warning would be enough and the bulletproof vest adequate backup. There was no shelter nearby, only a boulder more than fifteen yards away and halfway up the slope. Too far to get to in an ambush.

The roar of an engine had him swinging around. A snowmobile was almost on top of him. It was so close that he could only assume that the rancher had been lurking behind a stand of brush not far off the road. It was close enough that he would have heard every word.

"You've got some nerve!" the rancher yelled as he swerved in an arc, his rifle slung across his back, the machine spraying snow around him.

That was a relief, Zafir thought as he noted the position of the rifle. This time, for whatever reason, the rancher wasn't feeling threatened. Maybe his shouted introduction had had the hoped-for result, or maybe walking on the road instead of across his land had done it, or maybe it was a combination of both.

The man turned off the engine and got off the snowmobile. He spat, pulled his rifle off his back and strode toward him. The rifle, which replaced yesterday's shotgun, remained pointing harmlessly away from him.

The man wasn't very intimidating up close. He was small and wiry, his skin was wizened and browned by the sun, his hair was thinning, and only the edges held any remains of his former color, brown. He waved his rifle, using it more as a pointer than a weapon. "Didn't I tell you not to come back yesterday? Don't you know any English?"

"I'm with Nassar Security," he repeated, ignoring the questions and the intended slur. "The man you were threatening yesterday was my client."

"So?"

"A Moroccan royal," he said, as if that mattered, but sometimes more information soothed turbulent water.

"Bloody foreigner," the rancher snarled. "Send them back. Send them all back." He squinted at Zafir as if he'd just realized that he, too, might be foreign.

"Look," Zafir said through gritted teeth. It was an effort to not grab the sun-wizened sack of offal by the collar of his weather-faded jacket and haul him off the ground and give him a good fright. Instead he said with chill frosting his words, "I see you checked out the van. Find anything of interest?"

"Like what?" the rancher spat with an attempt at disdain, but despite the rifle, he'd taken a step back from Zafir.

"Any activity?"

"Another one like you." The rancher jabbed a thumb at Zafir, but he kept the rifle pointed at the ground. This time, though, his finger was on the trigger. It seemed an odd compromise.

"Like me? You mean Moroccan?"

"Yeah, whatever." He spat again.

"When?"

"Why would I tell you?" The rancher glared at him.

"Because I'll rid you of your problem once and for all," Zafir said in a low, confident voice. "He won't be showing up here again. Neither will I."

The rancher looked at him and seemed to consider whether there was any truth to that before he nodded.

"This morning. He was up to no good. In fact, he was gone as soon as he saw me."

"No good. What do you mean?"

"Nothing." The rancher spat. It seemed that he couldn't say more than a sentence or two before clearing his throat. "He left his trash." He pulled out a pack of matches and tossed them at Zafir. "Here. I have no use for them."

Zafir caught the pack one-handed and turned it over. The cover was embossed with the name of a well-known hotel in Rabat, Morocco. "Thanks for your time," he said with all the poise acquired through family pedigree and an Ivy League education.

"Don't forget you're still trespassing. I'll be watching." The rancher got on his snowmobile. He glared at Zafir and revved the engine. A minute later he shot across the road, heading toward the hills without a backward glance.

Zafir turned around with a thoughtful expression as he looked at the matches in his palm. "A Moroccan." He thought over that possibility, which now looked like it might be a probability. There were other Moroccans in Wyoming, like himself, he thought wryly, and two who had arrived recently. They knew where one was and it appeared that the other may have followed them here. It would be interesting to hear what Jade thought of it all and even more interesting to hear what she might have learned from Stan.

It was looking more and more likely that Stan had been followed by Mohammed Jadid from Rabat, Morocco, and then his cousin had attempted to kill him on foreign soil. He didn't believe in coincidence. It was unlikely that the explosion on Stan's uncle's estate and the attack on him here were unrelated. With the pieces of the case increasing, it looked more and more likely that they'd soon solve the puzzle. They had to, because without knowing the overall picture, they were shooting in the dark when it came to protecting their client. The drive back to Casper held an urgency that he hadn't felt since the case had been upgraded to code red.

## Chapter Fourteen

Jade was restless. She longed for action.

Behind her, Stanley sat at the table, a photography magazine in his hand.

"What do we do now?" he asked. He looked up at her as if he didn't have an opinion at all. "I mean where do we go from here?" He turned a page of his magazine.

"We can't stay here," she said. "You know that."

"I do," he replied. "I don't care what I promised. I can't stop thinking about going home." He turned another page of his magazine without looking at her.

"We talked about that," she said. "You agreed…"

"I know, but waiting isn't easy. I'd rather end this and go home."

"You could jeopardize your uncle by showing up out of the blue."

"How so?"

"There's someone after you here," she said, repeating what she'd told him earlier. Maybe it was stress, but he kept going back to the same need—to go home. "You're safe here, Stanley, in this place." She wasn't sure for how long, but they would be gone long before that ever became a problem. "They could follow you back to Morocco." She wasn't sure why she said *they*. There was only one person doing the shooting in Jackson; she imagined should they be followed, it would be one person again. The question was, who was that person?

"I never thought of that." He shook his head.

Even though she'd told him before, he hadn't remembered, hadn't heard—she wasn't sure which.

"Why does it have to be so complicated?"

"Money complicates," she said, thinking of the will. "Most of the time."

"I won't, just so you know," he replied. "Take off on you, and go to Morocco, I mean. But even saying that makes me want to jump on the first plane."

He turned to look at her, and she could see his frustration. He'd been confined to this small space for too long. She didn't give any thought to the fact that she had been stuck in this space, too, because it wasn't something that bothered her. She missed the adrenaline rush of the action, but she'd been in worse places, smaller places, on different assignments. It was a matter of distraction, taking your mind off the discomfort, which could turn into claustrophobia. Her own apartment was barely over four hundred square feet.

"On a completely different topic, if I'm not going immediately back to Morocco, then I'd like to take some pictures," Stanley said. "I mean when Zafir comes back, of course. Otherwise, we have no vehicle." His dark hair was mussed and he didn't look at her as she set a cup of coffee in front of him.

She'd scrambled eggs for him earlier, but if they were here much longer either she or Zafir was going to have to do a grocery run.

Rather than picking up his coffee, he stared rather morosely at it as if it were an alien entity.

"This hasn't turned out at all like I imagined."

She felt for him in that moment as his hazel eyes met hers, full of sadness and regret. For the first time she could totally relate to the man. Once, his worries had been about mundane issues; now he feared for his life and that of his uncle.

"I'm sorry you've had to face all this, Stanley. It's a little much for a layperson, but you've done fabulous." There was no point in mentioning the fact that he'd bolted and endangered himself further. That was in the past. "There's not many that would be shot at and remain as cool as you did."

He laughed. "I was scared to death and you know it."

She smiled back at him. "As far as taking pictures in the countryside, I'm not sure that it's safe. Whoever was trying to take us out in Jackson is still at large, and we have no identification on them."

"I know." He took a sip of coffee. "They're still out there. But we can't be squirreled away in here forever."

They didn't have a choice, because there were things he didn't know that he wasn't ready to know. She thought of his first cousin who was here and for only one reason that she could see: to kill Stanley. It was a guess and not confirmed by fact, yet. But she strongly felt that it was only a matter of time before he followed Stanley here, to their new safe house.

"No," she agreed. "But when we leave Casper we'll be able to function more normally and you can take some pictures. I promise. We'll get it all set up so that everything happens as close to what you planned as possible."

He looked slightly mollified at that information.

This time when he met her gaze, there was a look of guilt in his. Her intuition told her that the intimacy of just the two of them, the time that had passed since it had all happened and the revelation about his uncle might be the catalyst for a confession. Instinct told her that he knew a lot more than he'd revealed so far.

"Do you have any idea who was shooting at us in Jackson, Stanley? Do you have any enemies, someone who might want you gone?" She didn't add anything she already knew or suspected. She wanted Stanley to make his own pronouncement to prove once and for all that he trusted them. For without his trust, they had no ability to protect him short of locking him up.

"It would help us keep you safe, Stanley, if you would trust me."

She sat down across from him and put her hand over his. He looked down and then sadly back at her. He pulled his hand away and gazed at her for the first time as a man in charge of his own destiny.

"All right," he said gravely. "But you might not like what you hear."

"Try me."

He folded his arms, his brow furrowed as he sat back and a minute passed, then two. Then he began to speak. But the story that he told her had her wishing that there was something stronger to put into their coffee—for both of them.

But that wasn't an option. The new reality cast a dangerous shadow and put an edge to their case that hadn't been there before.

"It will turn out all right," she said.

"Keep it between the two of us," he said. "Don't tell Zafir, please."

"Stanley. I can't promise…"

"I know, but I don't want to be pressured into something when the truth comes out."

She could see his point. Zafir was strong and opinionated and could easily influence Stanley.

"I'll make sure he doesn't pressure you. But he'll obviously have some thoughts on what can be done, as do I. We only mean to make sure you're safe, and your uncle, too. If that means going back to Morocco, then that's what we'll do. But I'm not completely convinced of that. Let's just agree not to do anything rash." She met his dark eyes. "And that you trust us."

"Fair enough," he agreed. "I can't ask for more."

She wasn't sure if any of them could.

HE WAS BLOOD, and blood mattered. He'd believed that once, a long time ago. Now he knew that was a lie.

All that mattered now were the connections it afforded him so that he could go places and do things. For that, he needed money. Family connections were about to provide that for him, too. Best of all, family was going to allow him to play the ultimate childhood game. He'd get to torture Stanley one more time.

Stanley was nothing if not predictable. At least he'd been predictable until he'd come to the United States and hooked himself up with people paid to protect him. They'd been in Casper two days, and it had taken Mohammed that same amount of time to find them. Confined to that small apartment duplex, two of them and Stanley, who was used to living on his own and on his own terms; he couldn't imagine it. He would be going crazy by now rather like a rat in a cage.

He remembered how he and Stanley's brother had tormented him as a child. He remembered how they'd used his soft nature, his love of animals, to their advantage. But it was Stanley's brother who had taken that tormenting one step further. "By the ears," he'd say before he'd kick Stanley or better yet, a stray dog, for that was always guaranteed to set Stanley off more so even than his own pain. It was the first sign that things weren't quite right with Stanley's brother. But they got worse, much worse, and it was other, more brutal acts that finally had Stanley's brother locked up.

Time in what in those days had been called an asylum had only made Stanley's brother angrier. But it had made him no less violent. When the family had received the news notifying them of Chasi's death, he knew that it had been a grievous time for his aunt and uncle, but it had also been a relief. They'd been willing to believe anything that would relieve their pain.

Now, everything was working as planned; all he had to do was come through to get his promised share. One down and one to go.

He smiled. Now, with his uncle dead in the explosion in Rabat, Stanley had inherited, and with Stanley about to meet his maker and if he could succeed with the illusion that Stanley's brother might be back from the dead, and drive Stanley a little crazy, there was a fortune to be had. Illusion was everything. He was about to take his share; it was waiting for him right now in a Moroccan bank. As soon as the last act was complete and Stanley was dead, he'd get the code to complete the transfer. It was as brilliant as it was fragile, and Mohammed was more than glad to come along for the ride, do the grunt work and receive his lifetime payday. Now he only needed to finish the job and get out of the States as quickly and cleanly as possible.

When this job was over, he'd take the money he'd been promised and run far away so he'd never have to see Morocco again. He'd turn his back on it all, on all the craziness. The humiliation of his lack of status would never be an issue again. It was true, money could buy you anything.

## *Chapter Fifteen*

Shortly after Jade's conversation with him, Stanley went to lie down, claiming a headache.

Three quick knocks on the door. It was her and Zafir's agreed-upon alert.

She opened the door, and snow sifted into the small room, along with a blast of cold air that swirled around her ankles. She backed up. "It's gotten worse again out there."

"I can't believe this weather," Zafir said as he came in. He stomped snow off his feet. "Not that I'm surprised. In fact, I'd planned to do some snowboarding before all this came down." He smiled. "Faisal got me into it on the last trip." He took his boots off and then gave her his full attention. "What's up?"

"Sit," she said in a quiet tone. Knowing that his banter was only a screen in case their client was listening. "He's sleeping."

He came into the living area and sat down on the couch.

"Did you find anything at the van?"

His gaze roved over her like he knew her secrets. The thought of that sent a tingle through her that made her look away.

"There was evidence that someone else had been there. Not that that alone indicates anything, but the rancher gave me these." He held up the pack of matches from the Rabat hotel. "I went back to speak to the rancher and he confirmed that there was a man there who took off as soon as he saw him. In fact, it was earlier this morning. Ironically, I missed him by a matter of hours. He said that he was foreign and he was pretty sure that was who dropped the matches. He found them in the ditch. Anyway, Moroccan, I'd say from the look of these matches." He tossed the matches, and she caught them with one hand. "He also mentioned that the man was like me."

She looked at him with laughter in her eyes. "I'm betting, being the open-minded type he seemed to be, that didn't make him too happy."

"Not at all. Anyway, looks to me like we've only got one man after Stan."

"A Moroccan. Matches the airport security info," she said thoughtfully. "So he landed here and then made his way to Jackson following Stanley."

"He's our shooter?" she asked.

"Good possibility."

"The question is, where is he now?"

"And why does he want Stanley dead? Mohammed doesn't inherit. He has to have something to gain, but what?"

There was silence in the wake of the questions. They had no motivation, only too many coincidences.

"How'd Stan react to the news about his uncle?" He glanced over her shoulder to the bedroom where Stanley was snoring softly. "Did he finally come clean while I was gone? And told you not to tell me, too, I'm betting." He smiled, slow and lazy.

"He knew a lot more than we thought." She leaned back against the hard little sofa. There was a distance of only a few feet between them, and yet it seemed like there was no space at all. "In fact, it's a lot more complicated than we thought. He has the family from hell."

Zafir ran the back of his hand along his chin, where he had a good start on a beard.

She stood up and went to the window. Sleet drove in a white curtain, angling across the street and adding a white backdrop to everything. She turned from the window.

"Stanley revealed a lot while you were gone. He didn't want me to tell you," she paused. "I think you intimidate him."

"Enough to keep him in line," he gritted.

"We can only hope," she said with a smile. "Anyway, it appears he has a trust fund that he failed to tell us about."

"A trust fund?" Zafir looked at her with a frown.

"He claims it's recent and he didn't want it but his elderly uncle, who he apparently takes care of, insisted on it. One hundred and fifty thousand US dollars a year for life. All he has to do is continue to take care of the uncle."

"Explains the trust."

"Not totally," she said with a smile. "Seems Stanley is a dog lover. Promotes and donates any spare money he has to a dog rescue he supports. He's giving the majority of the trust to the rescue. And oddly, I don't think he knows anything of the inheritance."

"Doesn't know or won't admit?"

She shook her head. "I think he's telling the truth about that."

"So his cousin follows him here to kill him," Zafir said with a note of speculation in his voice.

"Possibly," she said. "Money aside, the interesting thing is the message on that phone, 'by the ears.' Turns out his brother was a sadistic…" She shrugged. "There's expletives that would fit but I'll leave it to your imagination until you hear the rest. Anyway, he'd torture animals often just to upset Stanley, who was an animal lover from way back. 'By the ears' was what he'd say to taunt Stanley before he either hurt him or a pet or another animal."

"So the message displayed on the phone is rather like a voice from the grave?" he said with a hint of irony in his voice.

"Possibly someone wants to have us believe that."

He nodded. "So we need to do some research on his brother's death. Maybe there's a connection we're missing. Another witness—something. What did Stanley say about it?"

"Not much. He was pretty young when it happened and, as we know, his brother had been confined to a psychiatric hospital where he eventually died. While Stanley originally told me it was an accident, he finally admitted that the family was told it was a suicide. There was no funeral and he has no official record. And we already know that there's nothing online. But the Marrakesh office has confirmed that there's a chart notation but no official record of his death in the institution where he died and that it was suicide"

"He died twenty-five years ago. That's a long time."

"It is and sadly I don't think there were many tears shed when he died. Before he was institutionalized, his brother's abuse was pretty horrific. Stanley claims that he still has scars. Sounds to me like his brother, Chasi, was unbalanced. I can't repeat all the stories, maybe Stanley can tell you, I… It's horrible."

"It's all right, Jade. If Stanley is up to it, I'll let him tell me. First hand is better anyway."

She looked at him with relief. "There's more. I mentioned the will, he claims to know nothing about it."

Zafir let out a soft whistle. "I think we need to have a long talk with Stanley.

After that, for a time, neither of them slept. There

was too much to consider, too much to reconfigure and consider again. But in the end, they realized it was Stanley who might have the answers, the final pieces of the puzzle, and his snores were still filling the small space.

Finally, as the night waned, they catnapped, in shifts, one taking over from the other.

It was an hour from daybreak when Zafir's phone rang.

Minutes passed before the call ended.

"They have a house that has everything we'll need. Thirty miles from here. The team is securing it now. It will be ready—" he looked at his watch "—later today."

"I hope we can keep him safe. That whoever—"

"Jade, it will be fine," he said, cutting her off. "Your success rate is one hundred percent. Any of our agents would kill to have you on their team, you know that," he said.

It was odd hearing the praise, for she knew that sort of thing was rare for him. There wasn't much she didn't know about him. And as she thought that, she missed the fact that he had closed the space between them. But those thoughts were pushed aside as he moved close, too close. His hands were on her shoulders, and she couldn't think or say anything. She could only instinctively respond to the hot need that erupted as his lips crushed hers. She knew that it wasn't in her power to stop him. She wanted this as much as he did, and all she could do was kiss him back. The kiss deepened, and he was demanding as much as she was wanting. It was a dance that was causing her body to tingle, her core to crave and her being to want more of him. Her breasts were crushed against the hard, toned wall of his chest. Her arms were around his neck. Her fingers tangled in the soft curls that wove seductively between her fingers. His tongue stroked the seam of her lips like an artist.

She melted deeper against him. She forgot all the reasons why she shouldn't do this, where they were, who they were...

It was the last thought that stopped her.

She pushed him away. Holy Hannah, this should never have happened, and it definitely couldn't happen again.

"Stanley," she reminded him.

"Is a name I'm beginning to dislike," he replied. The wry humor in his voice seemed to drift between them. But the space between them didn't cool. The hot, smoldering look he gave her said everything. It was as if he were willing to take her here and now as if... Her palms felt damp, and her heart tripped slightly at the thought of what she felt and what she suspected he wanted to do.

SHE TURNED AROUND and walked past him. Zafir watched her and really wished he hadn't for his gaze couldn't help going down to a perky butt that... That was twice he'd been caught by that part of her anatomy. He needed to pull his gaze away, to take his thoughts from the soft, rounded… It took everything he had.

Curves.

He wrapped his palm around the back of his neck as if a stranglehold massage would stop his thoughts. But his hand was only hurting his neck and doing nothing to stop the overwhelming awareness of her as a very attractive female. He wasn't sure what would help, but physical pain wasn't doing it. He dropped his hand.

He was unable to drag his eyes from her. Her figure curved in all the right places. He wanted to run his hands over her. He wanted to do so much more.

He couldn't.

He pushed the thoughts from his mind. They had a case to solve and a client to protect. He turned around, heading for the bedroom. He knew she'd gotten information from Stan, but after what he'd learned, he thought it was time they both sat down and had a long talk with him.

"Damn!"

Jade turned from the kitchen window and as she did, he met the question in her eyes. He stood in the doorway of their client's room, his fists clenched, all thoughts of passion or attraction forgotten.

"He's gone."

# *Chapter Sixteen*

Jade pushed past Zafir. The window was open; the blinds were rolled crookedly. A gust of wind knocked them back and forth. They hit the wall with a dull *clunk*, waited a second then two and then clunked again. It was like each *clunk* was reminding them of the danger. Her heart pounded so hard it hurt. Her mind screamed that this could not be happening again. She took three calming breaths. It didn't change the fact that he was gone.

Oddly, she didn't blame Stanley. They'd been here for too long; he'd been cooped up too long. He was tired of it. He'd told her about his disappointment and, at one point, even his heartache at not being able to take the photographs he planned. He'd also demanded to go home. But he'd given his promise, and that meant something to him, she knew that. He'd made that quite clear in the beginning.

"He's left a note," Zafir said. He held up a scrap of paper that looked like it had been torn from the cover of the magazine he'd been reading. "It says he won't be gone long. Don't bother looking for him."

"Don't bother looking for him?" she repeated, not sure that she'd heard right. "What is he thinking?" She couldn't believe that it had happened again. What had she needed to do, chain him to the bed? "We screwed up. Stanley's no ordinary inexperienced guy."

"Excuse me?"

"Inexperienced, yes. But we didn't factor in that he's royal," she said. "He has royal attitude. He thinks he can do things for himself, that he has that right."

"According to this note, he's left to do what he came to do," Zafir said. "He cites some advice you gave—as in manning up." There was a grim twist to his lips. "You said that to him? Don't you think that the lingo for one is rather, well, sexist?"

"Unfortunate wording. But it was just in the context of a long conversation, not as something he should do now," Jade said, striding toward the door. "I didn't expect…" She shook her head. "I told him that he needs to learn to be independent, it was part of manning up…" Sometimes she just talked, the words alone calming, and with Stanley that's what she'd done. And the truth was that they'd spent a lot of hours together, alone. She admitted now that there may have been things she'd said that would have been better left unsaid. But there was no going back.

"We don't have time to waste," she said. "We need to hit the street and get him back."

She strode back into the bedroom. She sensed or maybe just hoped that there was something else, something they'd missed, some clue. She stuck her head out the window.

She looked up and down the street, but there was no sign of Stanley. The only thing that was clear was the silence and the fact that the sun was just beginning to rise.

She looked at her watch. It was 5:45 a.m. Stanley had been gone less than an hour, because he'd come out to get a glass of water an hour ago.

"I should have seen this coming. I spent the most time alone with him." She gritted her teeth, pushing back from the ledge, but she was still reluctant to leave the window as if there was a clue there they'd missed.

"He had his camera with him," Zafir said.

She turned around. "How do you know that?"

"The dresser is empty except for his photography magazine, and that's where he kept it."

"I'm betting he wants a good picture of the aftermath of the storm at daybreak. I'm betting this is also his way of showing us that he can be independent. Take care of himself." She backed out of the room. "Could it be as simple as that?"

"So he jumped out the window to do so?" Zafir looked at her disbelievingly as he followed her out of the room. "Really? I think it's more likely he's going to leave town."

"Let's skip the airport run for now. He's had no time to book a flight, and I have his passport."

"You do?" he said with a smile. "Brilliant."

"Besides, my gut says that his intention is innocent. He likes to take photos in the early morning. Considering my earlier conversation with him, I don't think he's left never to return. He's not stupid. He's already felt what it was like to be shot at and to be on the run. I think he plans to come back. In fact, I'm positive. He knows he needs us."

"Convince me of that," he growled.

"There isn't any time. There's a good possibility that whoever tried to kill him in Jackson is here in Casper. This isn't a big place." She grabbed her jacket and headed for the door. "For now we go with the simplest option. That he's only taken his camera to take pictures. The best place for that, if you don't have a vehicle, might be the park that's not that far away."

"I hope you're right," Zafir said. "When I find him I'm going to…"

"Do nothing," she warned. "Unless you want him to bolt for good."

"Wait," Zafir said. "Before we go anywhere, I just want to say that this would have happened no matter what either of us would have said or done. Stan is stubborn. He's also a grown man."

"You're trying to tell me that it's not my fault?" she asked. She shook her head. "Thanks for that, but I wasn't blaming myself. I know he makes his own choices. We can only guide him. We can't make him follow instructions. Besides, this happened on both our watches."

A hand on her shoulder spun her around. Before she knew what had happened he was kissing her, hot and so sensual that she could only sink deeper into the kiss. It ended as quickly as it began. "Let's go," he said.

Zafir pushed the outside door open, and a rush of cold air met them.

Daylight was still just a promise. The snow reflected the glare of the streetlights and prevented the street from being completely dark. It was snowing again, and the flakes were sharper, colder as they bit and stung, and were quickly dashing away any evidence Stanley might have left behind.

Zafir looked up and down the street, but there was no sign of Stanley.

"He can't have gotten far. He has no transportation, and it's not as if there's a cab waiting outside," he said. In fact, the street was silent, the nearby houses still in darkness.

"He's gone to the park," Jade said. "I'm sure of it. He was determined to take pictures. He loves this time of day, or at least daybreak." They were walking toward the Pathfinder. Zafir opened the driver's door.

"There's nowhere else," she said. "Let's just hope he's alone."

There was no one on the street, and yet as the night thinned, it seemed that the danger only settled even deeper around them.

She clutched her gun as if it not only offered comfort and protection but answers. They didn't know who threatened Stanley's life. They only had theories but no facts. She was very afraid that Stanley had just walked into the trap of whoever wanted him dead.

"Stan might be naive and problematic, but one thing he's not going to be is injured or worse. Not on our watch," he growled. "If I have to tie him to my side."

"That might be our only option," Jade said, but already there was a sinking feeling in the pit of her stomach. "Let's move."

She took three steps and had her hand on the door handle. "If I'm wrong, the other option is exactly what you said, that he's halfway to the airport," she said. "He is resourceful."

"I trust your instincts. But I draw the line at resourceful," he said. There was an edge of humor in his voice. "He leaned pretty heavily on you at the airport," he said as he pulled out. "And he can't fly without his passport."

"Need I remind you that he's slipped our radar for the second time."

The look he gave her might have leveled a lesser person, but Jade had faced that and more in her lifetime.

He turned a corner and the Pathfinder slid as he pushed it just a little faster than conditions allowed. He steered it easily out of the slide without losing any speed.

They passed through a newer residential area where the snow-covered front lawns and houses with attached garages, front porches and bay windows all looked alike. There was no movement on the street; everything was quiet. Like the earlier block, the occasional house light was on; otherwise there was nothing. She had her eyes trained on the road, looking for Stanley or a sign that he had been here. But there was nothing to suggest that Stanley had come this way at all.

"You've got to agree," she said, "socially inept or not he's proven himself to not be a stupid man."

"I never thought he was. But I know what you mean. With the information we have at hand, we could never have expected what's transpired so far. It all seemed laid-back and easy, and to be fair, it was presented as such by Prince Rashad who contracted us in the first place."

"A false presentation. Neither Stanley nor this situation is any of that," she said, thinking of all she'd learned about Stanley in the time she'd known him.

Ahead of them was the park. It was five blocks

from the safe house. It was the only place within walking distance that was good for nature shots, the kind of photography that Stanley loved.

Zafir had turned off the lights before he pulled the Pathfinder over and parked. They were a half block away, a safe distance not to call attention to themselves.

Jade had been holding her gun with one hand. She put both hands on the Colt as if that were somehow reassuring. But in a way it was—she had a love affair with her gun that no one understood, at least no female in her life. She'd always had different interests. Her mother had once said that she'd make a better son than daughter. It was true, except physically, and that was the part that made this job a challenge. She didn't have the physical size of a man, and thus she had to rely on her wits, her self-defense knowledge and her skill with her gun.

"Ready," Zafir growled, breaking into her thoughts. "Hopefully this is where…"

"I see movement," she cut him off. "To the right. It's hard to tell. We're going to have to get closer. It could be anything, a stray dog…" But that seemed unlikely considering the neighborhood they had just driven through. It was a neighborhood where the dogs were designer and contained, not stray and unpredictable.

A flash of light streamed in a thin line across the snow and then was gone.

"A camera flash," she guessed, and gripped the

door handle with her free hand. "A good chance that it's Stanley. We need to go in."

"Not yet," he said. "I have a hunch."

Orders again. She gritted her teeth. She wasn't tolerant this morning. Maybe it was the fact that Stanley had managed to slip their protection for the second time. Maybe it was just because her head hurt from lack of sleep. But something felt like it was going to snap. She bit back what she wanted to say. This was no time for nitpicking. This was time to keep it together, to work together.

She ran her thumb along the barrel of her gun while her eyes swept the park. She glanced over to see that he had his gun in his left hand. But the casual way he was posed indicated that he wasn't so sure that the flash they'd seen was Stanley or that there was danger.

She wasn't so sure.

"Look," she said with a motion to their left. "We need to go, he's not alone."

The sun was rising and they could see Stanley just inside the park entrance. But it was the movement to his left, too distant to be clear, that had Jade concerned.

The unidentified man moved to Stanley's right. The sun was higher. There was enough light now for him to cast a shadow.

"Whoever is behind him means business. He's got a gun." She rolled down the window, prepared to lean out and shoot if necessary.

Both hands were on her gun, the weight of it almost a caress against her palm. Oddly a fleeting thought ran through her mind that the gun was a promise, a promise that it would not let either her or Stanley down. She leaned out through the open window, ready to go, to take it to the wall, shoot, kill, if necessary.

"We've got to go in," she said, knowing that the chances were slim that they could reach him unnoticed.

There was a glint of metal where the other man had slipped to the edge of a grove of shrubs. All they needed was for Stanley to turn. That could be deadly for him. But whether he turned or not, it didn't matter. The other man could only be after Stanley. She could see no one else in the park. It was a matter of time before he took him out.

*Stay focused*, she thought, as if somehow her thoughts could reach him. *Don't turn, whatever you do, don't turn.* She was afraid that if he turned it would trigger an attack. Right now the man shadowing Stanley seemed content to do just that.

"Hang on," Zafir said.

"What are you doing?"

"Providing a distraction."

He started the engine, the sound getting the attention of the men in the park, but before either could move, he'd gunned the engine and the Pathfinder spit snow as the tires spun. He let up on the accelerator enough to get traction. The vehicle bounced over the curb and into the park, moving fast enough that the two men had no chance to react immediately. Once they did, Stanley froze. The man shot at them, cracking the windshield.

"Down!" she screamed at Stanley. She was hanging as far out the window as she dared. She shot at the thin, dark-haired man holding the gun. The man who appeared to be stalking Stanley.

Missed.

"Get down," she screamed at Stanley again.

Stanley dropped into a crouch, his hands over his head as she fired again.

The other man shot once, twice.

Zafir slammed on the brakes. As the vehicle jerked to a stop they were both out, using the doors for protection.

Meanwhile, Stanley was on his knees and then crouched down and moving. He dived behind a hedge and was out of sight and immediate danger.

The other man had moved far enough away, using a grove of bushes on the opposite side, that it was hard to get a clear shot. As they moved from the vehicle to the cover of nearby trees, he bolted into the open, stopped, and then turned to shoot wildly at them.

Gunfire echoed through the park.

Something threw her off balance and she almost fell.

"Are you okay?" Zafir was there, covering her as he stood over her, gun in hand.

"I…" She looked down, expecting to see a gun-shot wound, blood—there was nothing. Only her jacket sleeve was ripped open. Otherwise, she'd been lucky. "I'm okay."

"You're sure?"

"Yes."

Zafir nodded. "I'm going after him. Get Stan out of here."

He grabbed her other hand and pulled her to her feet.

As Zafir took off at a lope after Stanley's attacker, she went over to where Stanley stood hidden in the midst of a thicket of shrubs.

"I can't take any more," he blurted out. "Why didn't you tell me that my own relative wants to kill me? My very own cousin. I can't believe this."

"Truthfully, we weren't one hundred percent sure until now and if we'd told you, I thought you'd demand to go home."

"You were right, and you wouldn't talk me out of it," he said quietly. "Uncle needs my help. I don't know what is going on but I don't like it not one bit. If I'd known, but I didn't recognize him until I was flat on my belly in the bush, watching."

"You were safe…"

"Was I?" He cut her off. "My cousin Mohammed comes out of nowhere trying to kill me. Why is he here?"

She had him by the arm. "I don't know," she said. "Something's very wrong. What's going on?"

"Let's get you out of here."

"I'm going home. I don't care what I promised." His lips were taut, and his eyes looked haunted. "I can't take any more," he whispered again.

She dropped his wrist and instead put an arm around his waist, as if somehow that would both comfort and contain him. "It'll be all right, Stanley."

He pulled away from her. "All right," he spat. "You call this all right. I've been shot at, hunted down like..." he stammered. "My cousin came out of nowhere and wants me dead." He laughed. The sound was dry and humorless. "Not that that is a surprise. He's hated me all my life. But why is he here?" His voice shook. "This is insanity. Craziness."

"The park's secure," Zafir interrupted as he joined them almost ten minutes later. He'd been running and he was breathing hard.

"I hit him once. Possibly twice. After that, he managed to elude me despite his injuries. Although I'd say that he's hurting badly. He dropped his gun. I've got it, so there's that."

"He's not armed," Jade said.

"Not that it matters much. I doubt if he'll make it. He's losing blood fast. It looks like an easy arrest or a morgue run," he said with a shrug.

Despite Zafir's harsh words, Jade felt no sympathy for Stanley's cousin. He was an assassin, more than likely a paid assassin. She just hoped that Zafir was right, that he was captured. She looked at Stanley. His expression hadn't changed. He didn't look shocked or saddened, just very annoyed. His cheeks were wind-reddened, his eyes bloodshot. The knees of his jeans were both ripped and his hair was mussed.

"I've notified the local authorities," Zafir said. "If he makes it, he'll need medical assistance. He shouldn't be too difficult to capture."

"Great," she said, and turned to Stanley. "Let's get you back to the apartment. It's freezing out here." She had him by the elbow as if preventing him from bolting again.

Stanley stopped at the edge of the park, pulled his arm free and looked at them with anger thinning his lips. "Look. I appreciate you saving my life, again," he said, contradicting everything he'd said before. "But I don't want a repeat of this. If I were you two, I'd drop this assignment while I was still in one piece."

He glared at Zafir. "Like I told Jade, I'm going home. This needs to end now. It's obvious that I'm the key to it all. I need to face whoever is orchestrating this. That's the only way it will stop."

Zafir said nothing, but he looked as if he wanted to wring Stanley's neck.

"Stanley," Jade said as she stepped between them. "For now, let's get back to the duplex." She took his elbow. "The rest can wait."

## Chapter Seventeen

They were a quarter of a block away from the park when they saw a man calling to a dog that was off its lead.

"Stop!" Stanley commanded in a voice that expected compliance.

"What's wrong?" Zafir asked even as he stopped.

"The dog's going to get hit," Jade said with horror as she saw what Stanley had seen first. She was out of the vehicle, just behind Stanley. Ahead of them, a border collie was in the middle of the intersection and a truck was wheeling around the corner. It was doubtful that the driver had seen the dog or that he would be able to stop in time. Stanley dived and in an unexpected move grabbed the dog, rolling out of the way of the truck, which honked as it swerved around them.

"Gotcha, boy," he said as he picked up the squirming black-and-white border collie.

"You might want to keep him on a leash until

you teach him to come when you call," he said to the grateful owner, who'd run up to claim his dog all the while thanking Stanley profusely.

"It only takes once and your dog is dead or seriously hurt," he said with an authoritative edge to his voice.

Jade and Zafir looked at each other. This was a completely different side of Stanley. He'd gone from near hysteria to determined rescuer in a matter of seconds.

"That's the other reason I need to go home," Stanley said five minutes later as he sat in the backseat for the short ride to the apartment. It was as if he'd read her thoughts. "The dogs need me. And I miss them more than I thought."

"Dogs? The rescues?" Jade guessed.

"Yes, I told you. Local shelter, I volunteer there. I use my nickname and what it's associated with. Like I told you, Stanley was a cartoon character. The program is well known in Morocco. It's nostalgia for the older generation, but they're bringing back a new version that's catching on with the younger set." He looked at both of them and seemed to sense that they weren't connecting with what he was saying. "Stanley—you know. Cartoon, funny. The name is well known, and I dress in character for various events. It raises money for the local shelter. Turned no-kill last year as a result."

Jade glanced at Zafir. Stanley was evolving from

socially inept royal to a man who was becoming more likable as time went on. It was hard not to like someone who had just escaped a harrowing experience and then had the compassion and foresight to save a dog's life.

Minutes later they were back at the safe house.

Stanley grabbed a can of Coke and sank down on the couch, slouching back as if his legs would no longer hold him. Zafir lounged by the doorway, his eyes on the window.

"I know I agreed to stay at least a few more days. I gave you my word, Jade. We shook hands, and that means a lot to me," Stanley said. And when no one spoke, his lips thinned and his eyes took on a determined sheen. "I know we talked about staying here just a while longer, and it made good sense then. But everything has changed."

He looked at both of them with an edge to his hazel eyes and a tight look to his usually full lips. "It's my money that's hired you," Stanley said, and neither one of them bothered to correct him, to tell him it was Prince Rashad. It was a moot point. "If I want to go to see my uncle, then I have that right."

"We'll discuss that later," Jade said firmly. "First we need all the cards on the table." She looked at Stanley. "Tell Zafir what you told me earlier."

Silence filled the room.

"Tell me what's going on," Zafir gritted out. "There's been enough foul-ups on this case."

"He already knows, Stanley," Jade said softly. "Fill in the blanks in your own words starting with the trust fund."

Stanley stood up. The expression on his face was pained. He folded his arms and then dropped them. He sat down, plopping heavily down onto the sofa.

"Uncle set it up for me. One hundred and fifty thousand American dollars a year for life," Stanley repeated what Jade had already told Zafir. "Some of that was for the rescue that I work with. He knew how important that was to me, and he used it as kind of a bribe." He shook his head. "I didn't want his money, but the truth is, the rescue desperately needed it." He worried his lower lip for a minute before continuing. "So I agreed. Although, except for the rescue, I would have gladly helped him for free. But the truth is that I need to work and couldn't devote myself to Uncle like he wanted. It was kind of a catch-22. So Uncle fixed it so I could." He laced his fingers together, his brow furrowed. "In the end, we reached an agreement that we could both live with."

"The trust," Jade added.

"Exactly," Stanley said.

"When did this happen?" Zafir asked.

"We discussed it a few weeks ago. He told me what he wanted and what he planned to do. I agreed and the final papers were signed just before I booked the flight here," Stanley said. "It was completely unexpected. I mean, when he presented the idea to me. But he's getting on in years and he needs help." He looked at them, with troubled eyes. "I've always been there for him, but now he wants me to live on the estate and take care of him full-time."

"That's a lot of money, Stan," Zafir growled.

"It is, but Uncle insisted. He wanted to help support my cause, and he didn't want to go to a senior facility or have strangers taking care of him. I don't mind doing it." He looked frightened and determined at the same time. "The trust is for the duration of his life, and it ends with either of our deaths."

There was silence. Zafir strode to the window as if there were answers outside the walls of the apartment.

Jade was beginning to feel a connection to Stanley that she hadn't felt for any other client. But then, he was different from any other. Young for his years and naive, but now showing another side, a more mature side and one she could admire. It was her job to ensure that he lived to act on the courage and caring he was showing now.

"That cottage, that's my bachelor pad," Stanley said. "I was supposed to be there for the last week. Then I decided to take this trip sooner rather than later. Especially with our agreement. Uncle wanted me to move in with him as quickly as possible. I wanted one more taste of being free and single."

Jade turned, knowing the shock was registering on her face. "You never told me that."

He shrugged. "I didn't think it had any importance."

"So, Stan," Zafir said. "It's safe to say that your cousin Mohammed followed you here intending to kill you."

Stanley frowned, and his eyes looked almost haunted. "I don't know why. What did he stand to gain?"

Zafir looked at Jade. She mouthed one word and he nodded.

"Did you know, Stan, that recently your uncle redid his will, and you're his beneficiary?"

"Me?" Stanley sounded shocked.

Jade looked at Zafir. It was clear that Stanley hadn't known.

"Your uncle didn't tell you?" she asked with quiet assurance.

"No. I..." His face reddened. "It's too much. I don't want..."

"You can deal with that later, Stan," Zafir said. "For now we need to figure out what is going on here. We know Mohammed has tried to kill you. The question is why?"

Stanley shook his head. "I don't know. Mohammed wasn't close to Uncle or me. In fact, he's not related to Uncle Khaled. He's from my mother's side. When he was a child he visited a lot, but always with his parents." He shook his head. "I don't want to talk about this."

"Keep going, Stan," Zafir snarled. "Some of this might very well save your life."

"Neither of us would choose the other as friends. As children we didn't like each other. As adults we haven't had much to do with each other. I don't know why he'd try to kill me now, after all these years." He stopped and worried his lower lip with his thumb.

Zafir's phone beeped.

"One minute," Zafir said, holding up his index finger as he stood up and moved into the kitchen area. "Yeah, Tara, what do you have, sweetheart?"

Jade watched as his expression changed from welcoming to grim in the space of two minutes.

Zafir put the phone in his pocket and came back to the common area, where he perched on the armrest of the couch as if poised to go into action.

"Tell us about your brother, Stanley," Jade said. She tried to ignore the fact that Zafir had just received information from that phone call. She could sense it from the look on his face and from the little she'd heard from his end. That would have to wait. It was critical that Zafir know everything that she'd so recently learned, because she sensed that they were running out of time.

"Everything, including what you didn't tell me."

He looked at her with surprise.

"No more secrets, Stanley."

She touched the back of his hand as if that would sway him, encourage him. "Start with the recent text message on your phone."

"By the ears," he said. "It was a horrid thing my brother would say to me when I was a kid. That phrase meant he was going to hurt me or hurt an animal I cared for. And I cared for them all, even the strays." He looked away.

She guessed that it might have been worse even than Stanley told her. She wanted to walk away, not hear it again. She had no choice but to stay.

Stanley dropped his head into his hands before looking at them again. "It was the one thing he shared with me and no one else. My brother, Chasi, was the only one who ever said that phrase, 'By your ears.' That message on the phone was like a message from the dead." His voice threatened to break. "Those words, they're like seeing him again. But he's dead, so who else knew?" He ran the back of his hand across his perspiring forehead.

"When you saw the message on your phone, you thought it was him right away?" Jade asked. "Even though he's dead?"

"He's been dead for twenty-five years. But I don't think anyone else knew he said that. It was our little secret." There was a quiver in his voice, and his hands were in fists. His face was white.

"He was close to your cousin Mohammed?" Jade asked.

"Sort of. As close as he could get to anyone." He nodded. "I can't believe it," he muttered. "You're insinuating that he's alive, that he hired Mohammed. Then where has he been all these years?"

"Did Mohammed spend time with Chasi?" Jade asked.

"Yes, he did. He visited and stayed over many times when I was young."

"And he would have heard Chasi taunting you, maybe heard that strange phrase of his?"

Stanley shook his head. "Maybe. I don't know. What does this mean?"

"I don't have any answers for you, Stan, but I bet there's still something you're keeping from us," Zafir said.

Stanley shook his head, his face flushed. Silence pulsed through the room before he began. The stories of torture and cruelty that followed were more than he'd revealed before, and Jade felt sick just hearing it.

"They said he was an uncontrolled psychopath. I was eleven when he was committed by my parents," Stanley said softly. "That's how they referred to it back then. Committed," he repeated. "I was relieved. My life got better after that."

Jade looked at Zafir. What Stanley was telling

them was unimaginable, but it was the classic pattern of a dangerous psychopath.

"What happened when your brother died? Is there anything that stands out in your mind?" Zafir asked.

"There was never a funeral." He shrugged. "At the time I didn't care. I remember that my father said that he thought something wasn't right. But there was never any proof of anything. I know my parents had no idea what went on in the asylum prior to his death. We had no contact after he was committed. Chasi refused to see either of them."

"There's no death certificate, is there, Stanley?" Zafir asked.

"I don't know about that. I've never looked," Stan said.

"Did anyone view the body?" Jade asked.

Stanley shook his head. "We never viewed the body, not that I know of. I had nothing to do with the burial, and I don't remember my parents attending, either. The hospital handled all of it, at least that I know of. I think my mother might have said a prayer or two. My father, he never spoke of him again."

"We just ran an official search," Zafir said. "There's nothing, Stan. As far as the Moroccan government is concerned, your brother's not dead."

He bit his lip and sank deeper into the couch. "It was all odd, everything about his death. At the time I didn't consider it much. I was too young to feel anything but relief. As far as the specifics, I never asked.

I was told that he committed suicide at the institution and that he's buried there. That's all I know."

The humming of the refrigerator was loud in the silence that followed.

"Who stands to gain from your uncle's estate if you're not alive?" Zafir asked. "Who is your next closest relative?"

Jade looked at Zafir, wondering where he was going with this. They'd received a copy of the will that named Stanley as beneficiary, but nothing that addressed who he would bequeath his estate to if Stanley predeceased his uncle. That was odd, and it changed everything.

"What are you suggesting?" Stanley's gaze swung between both of them. "I get the impression that you think my brother's not dead." His voice shook.

"Who inherits your uncle's fortune if you're dead, Stanley?" Jade asked again, softly. "Your uncle didn't specify a successor, so it would be his next closest relative."

"Uncle's not dead." His voice was ragged. "You told me…"

"He's not, but officially it hasn't been released who died when that cottage was destroyed. All they said was that an unidentified male died in that explosion. That's why it's so important to know who inherits next. Your brother might be a long shot, but we can't rule anything out."

The words hung between them as the seconds ticked by.

"If he were alive, Chasi would inherit, if how you say that will's written is right, if I were dead." He shivered.

"In the meantime, there's the trust. Who else knows about the trust?" Zafir growled.

Jade looked at him with a question in her eyes.

"The trust is evidence of a favored position. From it, one could easily assume that Stanley will inherit," Zafir said. "Even without knowing about the will. I'm betting that's why all of this has happened so soon. Someone got wind of what was going down."

"I think you're out on a limb on that one," Jade replied.

"And—" Stanley looked at Zafir "—in answer to your question, no one knows. At least no one was supposed to but…both of you and no one else." His voice broke. "Most of my relatives wouldn't care… they have money in their own right."

Silence filled the room as Stanley seemed to struggle to collect himself. "Now you see why I have to go home."

"I know," Zafir said. "And we'll get you there. But you won't be flying commercial."

"You'll be safe," Jade assured him, putting a hand on the crook of his arm as if somehow that would give him confidence.

He looked at her and smiled. "I know. It's about time I faced my brother."

"Let's not make assumptions, Stan," Zafir said. "Officially, for all we know—he's dead."

Two hours later, the company Gulfstream was waiting for them on the runway. It was only a matter of them walking to the plane that sat two hundred yards away.

"I don't like this," Jade muttered as they stood on the edge of the Casper airport tarmac. "I think we need a decoy. I'll go…"

"No," Zafir cut her off. "I'll go."

"We'll all go together," Stanley broke in. "It makes the most sense."

Jade and Zafir looked at each other. Stanley was full of surprises these last hours, showing intelligence, a touch of courage and a modicum of common sense. He wasn't quite the man they had first assessed him to be.

"Let's move," Jade said as she began striding out onto the tarmac with Stanley behind her and Zafir bringing up the rear. But as she turned, scanning the area, making sure that everything was clear both in front and behind, she could feel something was off.

A movement near a luggage cart had her pulling Stanley close, her other hand on her gun. She wasn't ready to make an overt show of force, not here at the airport. That would be asking for trouble.

A movement to the right, and she could also see

airport authorities moving around. No one was acting like there was any threat.

A luggage transporter moved slowly around a plane that idled on the tarmac. Seconds ticked by, and it was a full minute, then two, before either of them agreed to give Stanley the go-ahead. And as they did, a bag fell off a luggage cart, followed by three more. The noise made Stanley jump, and Zafir pushed past them so that he was in front, his hand ready to go for his gun. Jade grabbed Stanley, pulling him back between them. But it was nothing but what it seemed—falling luggage. There was no threat.

They were seeing danger everywhere.

## Chapter Eighteen

"I never thought that I'd get a chance to work in Morocco," Jade murmured. "I'd hoped, but... I suppose I wanted to arrive under better circumstances. I mean, a case, yes, but... Oh, never mind. I'm rambling."

"You're excited. It's refreshing," Zafir said.

They were already three hours into the last leg of the flight, having landed briefly at JFK before continuing their journey overseas. It would be close to eleven in the morning before they landed in Marrakech.

Stanley had fallen asleep an hour ago.

"What if his brother is exactly that, dead?" she mused, talking quietly on the off chance that Stanley might awaken.

"I've got Tara checking out the next living relative. Stan wasn't too sure about the cousins on his father's side." He scrolled through his texts as his phone beeped. Five minutes later they had their answer.

"Barring the possibility of his brother's death

being faked, the next in line is an unmarried cousin who hasn't set foot in Morocco in at least a decade."

"And…"

"From all appearances he has more money than he needs. He's enjoying a lavish lifestyle, and his main residence is in Paris."

"Interesting," she said, and they were silent, each mulling over this new possibility as the plane took them through the night of one continent and into the daylight of another.

"I don't like the thought of you in the thick of this," Zafir said.

"It's what I do," she replied. "Just like any other agent."

But his eyes said something else. She couldn't look away. It seemed the most natural thing when he leaned over and put a strong, sun-bronzed hand on her knee. It was too soon and too intimate, but despite that, something shifted between them.

His brown eyes were hot with desire. He looked over at Stanley. "If it wasn't for—" one shoulder rose, indicating Stanley near the back of the plane stretched out on a small couch "—I'd make out…"

"Make out?" she whispered. No man she knew would have used such an outdated phrase in such a teasing, yet tantalizing way. "Are you…"

He leaned over and silenced her with a kiss as he pulled her tight against him. She could feel his arousal pushing against her, and all she wanted was to give in to every ounce of passion she had for him. But this wasn't the place, not here on a plane with their client only yards away from them. It couldn't happen, and she wanted so badly for it to happen.

Her heart pounded, and something deep inside wanted only to melt into him. Her mind screamed to pull away. It couldn't be—this was the wrong time, the wrong place, the wrong man.

She put her hands on his shoulder, creating a suggestion of distance between them.

"Jade."

"No." She shook her head. For as much as she wanted him against her, as much as she wanted his lips ravishing hers, as much as she wanted all of it and more, she couldn't. Again, she pushed him away.

This was crazy, unanticipated and completely out of control. She'd never felt like this about another man, and he was completely the wrong man to feel this about. She knew his reputation. His track record was a train wreck for any woman. She looked out the window where the only thing to see were clouds. They were no distraction at all. She had to get it together.

She didn't want any of this. At least, that's what she told herself. It was as if telling herself would control the feelings that were wild and difficult to contain. They were completely different from anything she'd felt with any other man.

He was like no man she'd ever known, even

though he was an identical twin. She'd met Emir on one of his visits stateside. There was no comparison. For one, Zafir's handsome face bore a scar that ran the length of his left cheekbone to his jaw. It did nothing to distract from his good looks, but it made him even more rugged-looking than his twin. But it went deeper than that. Zafir had an aura about him. He angered her like no other, and yet she felt physically safe in his presence and emotionally wrecked, for he was too hot, too passionate and altogether too dangerous.

He was proving all that now. Making her pulse with need, making her want to bridge the distance between them and pick up where she'd forced him to leave off—where she'd ended it. But it needed to be ended. It could never be. Her thoughts needed to straighten out. They were confusing and cloudy, almost dizzying. What was important was Stanley and his safety. They needed to secure him and make sure he was safe. What had just happened couldn't happen again.

"Let's go over our plan when we land," she said, but her lips were sensitive from his brief kiss, even as her belly fluttered. She was aroused in a way she hadn't been in a very long time. Her body was acting out of sync with her mind.

Zafir headed to the front of the plane, where he grabbed a bottled water for each of them from a compact fridge. He came back a few minutes later. His hand settled on her shoulder. "You're hot," he whispered in her ear.

His words, his nearness, had heat running through her. She wanted him. She needed to pull back.

"Like no woman I've ever met before."

He slid into his seat and picked up the file as if he had said nothing at all.

She was a puddle of molten attraction, trying to regain control. She needed to rein it in, and apparently, she needed to rein him in, as well. And yet at the same time, she only wanted to fall into his arms and let nature take its course.

So much for reining anyone in.

She wasn't sure how this would all turn out. When the assignment was over, would his feelings be gone? It was no secret that Zafir was a love 'em and leave 'em kind of guy. His broken trail of romances was evidence enough of that.

"What's with the look?" he asked.

His eyes were alive with desire. They seemed to take all of her in. If she said the word, if there were no Stanley—she knew exactly what they'd be doing on the butter-soft leather of a private airplane seat while they continued uninterrupted on their journey through the skies over the Atlantic.

Morocco.

Somehow that one word, a place where she'd never been and where she was about to land in just a few hours, brought reality slamming back into focus like nothing else could.

She met his gaze with steely determination. This was it. This was business, nothing more.

The tablet dinged a warning that a message had arrived. It was the second call to reality.

Now, the passion was gone, and instead that dark drive to close this case successfully was there—a seriousness that replaced the passion in a split second. She turned her attention to the tablet, skimmed her thumb along the screen, looking at the latest information that had come from the admins in the main office in Marrakech. It was rather an enlightening piece of information.

He looked backward as if to ensure that, despite the snoring, Stanley wasn't feigning sleep.

The plane hit a patch of turbulence and the interior cabin lights blinked.

"Fayad el Eloua, the only remaining nephew besides Stanley and one year younger, has just recently returned from Paris to Morocco."

He looked up. "That's interesting."

"Could the possibility of an inheritance have brought him back?"

"The research says that he inherited his family's wealth and lives a lavish lifestyle." He looked up. "Tara passed it on for an investigation into his bank accounts. She doesn't have the means to access something like that."

"You don't think…"

"Stanley's brother was always a long shot," he said. "But still can't be discounted."

The lights blinked, and the small silver communication box beside Zafir buzzed. He picked it up and nodded as he listened. A message from the pilot, Jade guessed, as she watched him receive whatever the message was through the earbud he was wearing.

"It'll be rough for the next few minutes," he reported to Jade while standing up to dim the lights over the still-sleeping Stanley. "He's buckled in," he said in a whisper. "Best get seat belts on ourselves."

She looked over at Stanley. "He's not used to what's happened in such a short period of time. But he's adapted amazingly well."

"He has," Zafir said, balancing easily as the plane jumped again before sliding into his seat and fastening his seat belt.

"We need the landing site secure," Jade said. She wasn't sure why she was stating the obvious.

Zafir ran a finger along her cheek, pushing a strand of hair back from her face, his touch velvety soft and hot. "It's secure," he said in a whisper that made his deep voice so gloriously seductive that it was impossible to focus on what he was actually saying.

She was doomed. Her growing feelings for him were impossible to put aside.

His dark eyes grazed lazily over her.

"What about my gun?" she asked, needing the distraction of something else.

"Royal sanction," Zafir said. "Our agency is authorized as part of our doing business."

He looked at her with surprise, as if accusing her of asking pointless questions for answers she already knew. He was right. She had been trying to divert the hot tingle of desire that was fudging her ability to think her way clearly through this case.

"We're two hours from landing. That's all the time we have to make sure the plan will be something we can get Stanley on board with," Zafir said.

"That's the key, isn't it?" Jade murmured as she took a sip of water and glanced at Stanley, who had only changed position but was still sleeping soundly. "A plan that will keep Stanley safe and one he's happy enough with to consider cooperating."

"In any other situation an easy task," Zafir said as he looked at her, this time with the passion of a challenge in his eyes. "But we've known that from the beginning."

"Let's do it, hit this thing with boots on the ground," she said with relief, her mind finally on their mission.

"And a cooperative client," Zafir said with a smile.

"And that," she replied.

They worked together like they'd done it for years, and in the end what they came up with, there was no question that Stanley would cooperate. They both agreed that there was no way he could not be happy.

He would soon be in Morocco, with his uncle and his beloved rescue dogs.

Now they only had to keep him alive.

# Chapter Nineteen

Zafir's brother Talib was there to meet them at the Marrakech airport as they emerged into a private area.

"Good to see you, bro," Talib said as he clapped Zafir on the shoulder. "You lucked out. Emir and I have been running back-to-back cases that have been keeping us in Marrakech. Otherwise, you would have been on your own."

"Jade." Talib turned to her before anyone else could say a word. He offered her a smile that was solid and genuine. "Good to see you on this side of the ocean."

He held out his hand, which she shook warmly, and then he turned to Stanley, shaking his hand.

"I'm between cases," Talib said, leading the way out of the airport. They moved through a private corridor that was closed to most passengers and outside to a private parking lot. "Just got back from checking out a hotel."

"You're going into the hotel business?" Zafir asked with a laugh.

"As if," Talib said. "I'm trying to convince a friend of mine that it's a bad idea. But he's determined. If the deal goes through, he has me lined up to make sure the security is up to par."

Zafir's phone beeped.

"Your cousin Mohammed won't be a threat to you again, Stan," Zafir said a minute later.

"He's dead," Stanley said flatly.

Zafir nodded.

A look of relief washed over Stanley's face, but it was fleeting. He looked at Zafir. "It was your gunshot?"

"Unfortunately, I believe so," Zafir replied.

"Not unfortunate at all from all you've told me. He was no good." He took a deep breath. "I have to go to Rabat immediately."

"Your uncle's estate," Jade said. "That's…"

"We'll get you there." Zafir cut her off with an edge of impatience in his voice.

Jade gave Zafir a quelling look. One minute he was turning her on and the next he was pissing her off. Right now she was getting tired of his take-charge attitude. She didn't miss the amused look Talib gave them both.

"Now," Stanley said, redirecting her attention to him as he stopped and put his suitcase down, as if that made some kind of statement.

She went over to Stanley and took the handle of his suitcase, preventing him from picking it up without wrestling it from her hand. "You trusted us in Wyoming?"

"Yes. But…"

"We've got your back, and we know you need to get to Rabat." She looked at him and saw tears glistening in his eyes. "And we'll get you there. But we're going to make sure you're safe in the process."

"He's the closest thing I have to a parent. There is no one else. What if he's in danger?"

"He's fine, and we'll be there soon. This afternoon."

Stanley picked up his suitcase. "Okay." He nodded at Talib. "Let's do this."

A minute later they were getting into Talib's Jaguar. "British Racing Green, that's the color it's called," Zafir said with a laugh at her look of awe. He winked at her. "Talib loves luxury sport vehicles."

"Not more than he loves speed," Talib said, laughing. "Fasten your seat belt, folks."

The car was luxury on wheels, and Talib flirted with speed limits as they made their way into the heart of Marrakech and the asylum that had once held Stanley's brother.

Twenty minutes later, Talib rounded a corner and took them through a massive set of gates that looked like something out of the Middle Ages. The drive was wide and lined with palm trees, which made the whole approach rather strange, like they were entering a resort.

The asylum was old. It was built on the edge of the medina, where ancient walls separated the city's oldest neighborhood, once a vibrant trading center, with its narrow twisting streets, packed with vendors and shoppers, from the rest of the city. But despite the busyness of the area, the psychiatric hospital that had once been called an asylum stood alone on large grounds that gave it a feeling of isolation. It had been built at the turn of the twentieth century. Now the old facade remained, as well as the ten-foot wall of sun-bleached brick complete with a two-foot topping of barbed wire. It was a modern-day reminder of pain and suffering, but inside she knew that it had been completely changed. A fully modernized hospital now occupied the majority of the grounds.

The exterior, despite the fact that massive renovations had been done, was less inviting than a modern prison. The question that lay in all their minds was if Stanley's brother, Chasi el Eloua, had left those walls alive or if he had died as claimed twenty-five years ago.

Stanley had his hands laced together, and his jaw was tense.

"You don't have to go in," Jade reminded him. "Talib will stay here with you."

Stanley nodded, a grateful look on his face. "I'd

prefer that," he whispered. "I've never been inside, and I'd like to keep it that way."

"I understand," Jade said, and she did, for she was also feeling reluctant to enter this grim-looking facility. She'd never been a fan of hospitals, having seen her father in one as a child. He'd died in palliative care of a neurological disease that had taken two long, drawn-out years. It had left a lasting impression.

"In fact," Zafir said, "why don't we meet you in the medina." He clapped his hand on Stanley's shoulder. "Maybe you can find a gift for your uncle in one of the souks," he said, referring to one of the numerous marketplaces within the walls of the medina. "I believe there's a souk just a few blocks away."

Stanley brightened. "It would take my mind off of this," he said.

They waited until Talib and Stanley pulled away before heading toward the building.

"The employee the administrator referred me to is particularly knowledgeable about the earlier cases, those that aren't online," Zafir said.

She followed him as he turned to face the entrance. Like the rest of the outside, here the facade of age masked the modernized core of the psychiatric hospital.

"Are you okay?" he asked.

"Why shouldn't I be?"

"You don't like hospitals. I've read your file, Jade. I know it wasn't a good way to lose a parent."

"We've both had bad experiences. It was a long time ago. I'm fine, really," she said. She was shocked that he knew that much about her, that he cared enough to check it out and mention it, to make sure she was all right now.

"Then let's go," he said as he led the way through the doors where inside, they were overwhelmed by the liberal scent of disinfectant.

"The older section is no longer used, and there's a new area dedicated to psychiatric beds," Zafir said.

"Interesting," she replied.

"Is it?"

She stopped. "What do you mean?"

"That it has no relevance to the case. I was only making conversation."

His phone buzzed. "Wait," he said to Jade and took the call. A minute later he disconnected from their Marrakech office with a troubled expression. "Seems the bank records for Fayad el Eloua are looking grim."

"Broke?"

"Pretty much. Unless he's hiding it elsewhere there's not much left."

"That could change everything." She took in her surroundings. "Or so could this."

They approached the receptionist, who passed them on to another employee, who then passed them off to a young woman in a white lab coat.

Jade was intrigued as they walked briskly through

a gleaming off-white corridor. It was as if they'd been dropped from archaic to modern in the space of seconds. The sleek lines of the updated area seemed to clash with the ancient brick and stone of the exterior they'd just seen.

"Even upgraded, it isn't very inviting," Jade whispered.

They stopped at an elevator. Jade crossed her arms and warded off a shiver.

"You'll find Omar on the basement floor in the southwest corner. He's our longest standing employee and considers himself our unofficial archivist," their guide said in Arabic. "Actually, we all do. He has more information stored in his head than we have in the records room," she said with a light laugh before turning to leave.

Zafir repeated the information in English to Jade.

"This is a problem, isn't it? Me not speaking the language."

"Let's hope we're not here long enough for it to be a problem," he said as the elevator doors shut. "Although there are many people who speak English or French, as well."

The elevator doors opened, and the musty smell of basement met them. Jade wrinkled her nose. For a second it felt like the past had wrapped a shroud around them. As they stepped out into the hallway, it was clear that the modernization had stopped in the basement. While the concrete walls had been painted white, the tile on the floor looked well worn. A battered gurney was against one wall as if it had been forgotten there and an exit sign glowed red at the end of an endless length of hall. They turned away from the sign and down the corridor in the opposite direction. Light filtered from a doorway and lifted some of the gloom. Just ahead of them a thin man stepped out of the shadows.

"Are you Omar?" Zafir asked and at the man's nod, he said, "Zafir Al-Nassar and this is Jade Van Everett."

Jade was surprised at how young he appeared. The only sign of the fifty years they'd been told that he'd worked here was his graying hair and a rather stooped posture, as if he'd sat at a desk too long. Although, she knew that wasn't the case as they'd been told that the majority of his work experience had been menial.

They both shook his hand, and he ushered them into a large room that was filled floor to ceiling with steel shelving holding boxes of files.

"Most of this has yet to be put online," he said with a wave of his arm. "You asked about Chasi el Eloua. He was committed a long time ago. But I'll never forget that case. It was the worst I'd seen at the time. Everyone talked about it."

"Worst?" Jade asked. "How?"

"He was violent, so violent. He had no empathy for anyone or anything. He didn't try to hide it, either.

I'd never seen a patient like him. What the family told us was terrible. But here, it seemed to get worse. You couldn't turn your back on him. He broke an orderly's arm and hospitalized an aide the first week he was here. In fact, for his first months he was locked up in solitary confinement and, because of similar violence, off and on over the years that followed."

He shuffled through a box of papers and then turned around, scanning the room as if he'd lost his train of thought.

"You said you had proof of his death?" Jade interrupted.

He nodded. "He committed suicide, but not before threatening the lives of two staff members and fatally wounding two of the other patients. He partially beheaded one of them. I've never seen anything like it."

"How?" Jade asked, horrified at what she was hearing.

He shook his head. "Somehow he managed to escape his cell. Then he stole a carving knife from the kitchen. It took three of us to get control of the situation." He shook his head. "I was one of them. We weren't able to stop him from jumping from the fifth-floor window."

"You're sure he died?" Zafir asked. "That it was him?"

"No doubt," the man said. "I've had a lot of positions in my time. Then, I was in charge of removing the body and cleaning the cobblestones after." He shrugged. "It wasn't an uncommon chore."

He looked at each of them. "I'm sorry, that must seem harsh. Anyway, I was here when his father came to identify him." He looked at both of them. "There was no doubt that he was dead. As far as the legal registration, I don't know what happened there. It isn't a first, though, at least back then. So it doesn't surprise me. But one thing I can guarantee is that he was and is dead. A sad ending, but then maybe it was for the best." He handed them the chart. "See, it's notated here as I'm sure administration told you."

Zafir looked at the notation, and then glanced at the notes that proceeded it. There wasn't much there. In fact, what Omar had told them said so much more. "Date and time of death is here in the chart. That's about it," he said to Jade.

"Did he ever get visitors? From family or anyone else?" he asked Omar a few minutes later.

"Family, no, never. Except that one time for identification." He paused. "He refused to see his family. No one came that I know of in the entire time he was here."

"Thank you," Jade said as they shook hands and left.

THE VISIT TO the hospital had taken them less than an hour. Still, it was a relief to be away from the dank smell of the basement and the haunting remnants of lives destroyed by illness and outdated ideas about treatment.

Jade took deep breaths, as if that would remind her of life and hope. The hospital basement, the story of Chasi's sad ending, was haunting. It was impossible to forget that nightmare and it made her consider briefly what other horrific stories might be contained within that hospital.

"Stanley's cousin Fayad el Eloua is in financial straits and conveniently, he inherits if Stanley is out of the picture," she said as they walked. "I don't like the sounds of this." They crossed a narrow street and turned right, entering the medina, where it was mostly only pedestrian traffic; the streets were walled in and narrow. The buildings crowded close where the walls didn't. As they neared the souk, the street became more congested. Merchants and goods crowded on both sides. Tourist trinkets and local goods wove together as one shop seemed to merge into the next.

"Fayad might still believe that his uncle is dead. Information to the contrary hasn't gotten out yet, but I'm betting that if he doesn't know about Mohammed's death, he will soon," she said. "That means he will know that Stanley is alive. And he can track him here."

"I think from here on in we don't let Stan out of our sight."

"I agree," she said as she strode beside him.

"Talib just texted," Zafir told her. "They're waiting for us. We'll helicopter in to Rabat."

They walked the remaining block to the heart of the souk in easy silence. Although Jade found that her mind kept going back to the grim hospital basement and Chasi's last moments. They were a distraction. But the thoughts were soon driven away by the intoxicating scent of incense and spices. The warm scent of cinnamon laced through the sharp tang of cloves and the heavier scents of curry and turmeric. The noise of a multitude of voices and activity became an unidentifiable hum. As they got closer, the volume increased, and it was impossible to hear what each other was saying without shouting, so they walked in silence. The merchants had bordered the narrow street with their wares sprawled out in front of them, but now they entered an area crowded with both tourists and locals. Vendors and their goods lined one stall against another. There was motion and color and noise wherever they looked. Colorful robes hung from one stall, a brilliant display of scarves hung from a second and souvenir T-shirts at another. Barrels of spices were lined up in the next. A woman called to them, motioning them to come to her stall, to check out the red-hued pottery that was spread out in front of her. Across from her, another pottery seller also called to them. Her pottery hung from hooks, pitchers in vibrant colors and pots around her feet. A man in a beige-and-white-striped djellaba guided a donkey with woven baskets that bulged with red and yellow cloth. The merchants were crowded into the narrow space, many dressed traditionally, a few in modern attire. For a moment the smell of manure wove through the rich scent of spice, and oddly wasn't off-putting. She stepped sideways, dodging a donkey's fresh leavings.

"We're meeting Talib at the Spice Haven. It's owned by a friend of the family. The shop is another block from here," Zafir said.

A few minutes later, a woman pushed between them. Jade was jostled from the other side and turned to catch up with Zafir. In that moment they were separated by a man leading a pair of donkeys and a group of women who pushed ahead of the man and his animals.

A sinewy arm wrapped around her waist and yanked her backward. She was slammed back against someone. She couldn't see behind her. She could only hear rough breathing as she was dragged backward, to the edges of the crowd.

Just like that, she was pulled out of the main corridor of traffic and into the fringes. Here, transactions were made, of people, goods, animals, that went on unseen every day, in the shadows. Here, kidnapping and murder would slip by unnoticed. She had to get away. She needed a distraction. More than likely, she would have only one chance. She didn't fight. She wanted to let her captor think she was resigned, passive. She had a glimpse of Zafir twenty feet ahead of her. He was boxed in in the midst of the crowd.

A heavy hand clapped over her mouth, jarring her teeth against her lips. She took a breath, smelled stale sweat and without hesitation sank her teeth deep into the sweaty flesh. At the same time, she brought her heel down on his instep, her hiking boot slamming as hard as it could into the soft cloth of a sneaker. Luck was on her side. She broke free as her attacker cursed and eased his hold.

Through the crowd she looked sideways and could still see glimpses of Zafir. It was doubtful that he could see her, she was blocked by her captor. There was no time to contemplate that or anything else. To do so would be to lose the edge she now had. It was act now or never. She pulled her gun all the while knowing that she wouldn't use it in such a crowd except as a desperate measure, but her attacker didn't have to know that. She looked into his rheumy brown eyes and saw the disconnect she saw in many killers. This man saw her as nothing of value, as a thing, something to be removed in whatever fashion it took.

"You won't kill me," he snarled.

A shout just to her left. She was distracted for a split second, but that was all it took. He grabbed her left arm. She couldn't free it; instead she swung with her right, the one holding her Colt. She slammed the butt of the pistol against his temple. His grip loosened. Suddenly, she was completely free and her attacker was yanked off his feet. Zafir had one of the man's arms twisted behind his back. His other arm was crushing his windpipe. He looked over the man's shoulder, looking straight at her as if she was all that mattered, as if a filthy man with murderous intent did not stand between them.

"You're all right?"

She nodded. "Let's get him contained," she said as she pulled out a set of handcuffs.

Their captive cursed in Arabic.

Zafir answered him in Arabic.

"He wished me an unpleasant death, in not quite those terms," Zafir told her. He didn't say what he'd said in reply. She imagined it hadn't been friendly.

She snapped the cuff on the man's thick yet sinewy wrist. He spat, his dark hair glistening with grease, the scent of sweat clashing with the exotic smells that had been so enticing earlier, and the combination made her stomach curl.

"Over there." She pointed six feet to her left where there was a metal flagpole, held upright by a block of cement.

Zafir dragged the man with his arm tight around his neck. Her attacker didn't have a choice—either cooperate or choke. At the flagpole, he glared at her.

Jade gave the cuff on one wrist a hard yank. The man pulled back, refusing to get close enough to have the cuff close on the pole. Zafir was about to step in when she took their captive's legs out from under him with a hard kick to the back of his knee. He fell as she snapped the cuff onto the pole.

"Who hired you?" she demanded.

He spat. An expletive that was clear in any language followed. But he refused to look at her.

She lowered her gun, aiming for his crotch. "Five seconds." She warned. "One…"

"I wouldn't push her," Zafir said as he moved beside her.

She didn't take her eyes off the greasy character in front of her. He was a classic criminal for hire, not above doing anything sleazy, not smart enough to come up with the crime himself but more than willing to collect money for any number of acts. He glared at her, his thin lips tight with disdain.

"Three."

"Fayad el Eloua."

"Where is he?" she asked. "This time I'm not going to count." She brought the gun a few inches lower, a few inches closer.

He placed his hands over his crotch as if that would somehow make him bulletproof.

Behind her, Zafir chuckled. "I wouldn't want to be in your place," he said, but his voice was low enough that Jade doubted the man had heard.

"Where?" she repeated.

"I don't know," he gritted. "I was supposed to meet him in Rabat in two days."

"Where?"

He named a hotel in Rabat.

She turned around.

Zafir was on his phone, but he nodded at her. She stepped away from their captive as Zafir ended the call.

"The police will be around to release you," he said as he disconnected. "Although I doubt there will be much releasing happening. Maybe a ride to the cell block."

The man snarled and cursed.

Zafir looked at Jade. "We'll have this trash picked up in no time."

A man began to clap, and a woman whistled as if they thought this was a play put on specifically for them.

"Time's running out," Jade said to Zafir. "Let's get moving."

# Chapter Twenty

"Security found a breach at the Marrakech Menara Airport," Zafir said. "A mechanic alerted Fayad el Eloua of Stanley's arrival. From there it was a series of informants marking our path all the way to the psychiatric hospital."

"He's resourceful," Jade said. "The question is, where is Fayad now?"

"That's what we don't know. What I do know is we need to get Stan's uncle out of there and keep both him and Stan close until we get this man contained."

They were standing on the edge of his family's compound in Marrakech. In another circumstance, Jade would have been in awe. The grounds were massive; behind them an infinity pool stretched, seeming to touch the distant edges of the mansion that was the family home. As it was she only noted the details and focused on the helicopter that would take them to Rabat, where they could make sure that Stanley's uncle would live out his remaining years.

They took off ten minutes later from the Al-Nassar compound. Zafir flew them in while Talib took the copilot seat. If anything went wrong, it was agreed that Talib would be getting Stanley and his uncle out.

Nothing would go wrong, Jade thought. She clenched her hands in her lap. And even as she thought that and glanced at Stanley to make sure he was okay, she knew that they couldn't assume anything. They didn't know where Fayad el Eloua was. He'd rented a rattrap apartment in one of the poorer areas of Rabat. Whether or not he was there now, they had no idea. The first priority was securing Stanley and his uncle.

No one was saying much. Everything that could be said, at least in front of Stanley, had been said. Instead, Jade watched Zafir's easy maneuvering of the aircraft. It didn't surprise her that he was an accomplished pilot. She wondered if there was anything that he wasn't accomplished at.

"Stint in the Moroccan air force," he said, glancing back at her, answering her unasked question.

"I didn't ask," she said with a laugh.

"But you thought it," he replied as he steered the helicopter into a turn, dipping it slightly to the right. "Even without that, I probably would have acquired my license. It's kind of the family path. Each of us learns to fly and joins the business."

"Tara?" she asked, referring to his sister.

"Maybe. Someday," he said with a smile.

"Never," Talib said.

She turned to look at Stanley. "Have you managed to contact your uncle yet?"

"He's not answering," he said. "But he said when I spoke to him earlier that he'd be here waiting for me. He was looking forward to a visit."

"I don't like it," Zafir said. "You said there was no answer from our agent on the estate."

Talib nodded. "I'll try again."

"Uncle could be in trouble, is that what you're saying?" Stanley asked.

"No," Zafir said.

"What don't you like?" he persisted. "What does it mean?"

"It means you should stay in the helicopter while I get your uncle and fly you both out," Talib said. "Jade and Zafir are well equipped to deal with any trouble."

"You mean my cousin? Is that the trouble?"

"No," Talib said patiently. "I mean exactly what I said. Any trouble."

"My cousin Fayad," Stanley muttered. "I haven't seen him since I was a boy. I remember he was distant even then. I thought he was living the good life in Paris. That he was like all my relatives, most of them, anyway—rich."

"He kept up a good illusion," Jade said.

They arrived in Rabat at three in the afternoon and landed in a small field a mile behind the stone mansion Stanley had told them about during the flight. It had all gone exactly as planned. Except that not only was their agent not responding, but a third call to the mansion went unanswered. The estate seemed deserted. The land seemed to breathe silence.

It was clear even from this distance that something was wrong.

"Get Stanley out of here," Zafir said to his brother. "I don't like any of this."

Talib nodded. It was the first rule of Nassar Security to protect those you could as quickly as possible. Otherwise the damage could amp up, fast.

"My uncle?"

"Will leave with Zafir and me, Stanley," Jade said. She only hoped that was the truth.

"Promise me," he said as Talib took his arm, keeping him at the helicopter. He protested again, weakly this time, for it was clear even to him that Talib was not beyond using more force than he already was.

"SOMETHING'S NOT RIGHT," Jade said. The helicopter had taken off with Stanley and Talib over fifteen minutes ago. Now she was crouched fifty feet from the main house near an outbuilding. Ahead of them was the remains of the stone cottage, and between that and the mansion stretched silence.

Seconds turned into minutes. The estate seemed to be empty, and that was warning enough that there was trouble. Unidentified trouble, the worst kind.

"Get down!" Jade barked at Zafir, getting lower and moving in his direction even as she scanned the area and motioned with a flick of her right wrist.

A shot rang out from somewhere near their right and closer to the mansion.

"Split up," Zafir said as he waved her farther away. Later, he'd regret that command. He'd regret it for the rest of his life. For now, he was concentrating on keeping them alive.

Another shot kicked dirt up a few feet from where he was sheltered behind the tires of a small tractor. He moved deeper into the yard and closer to the mansion where they suspected Stanley's uncle was. Jade had moved ahead of him and was using a small shed for cover.

But the closer they got to the mansion, the more broken and rusted farm implements they found. It was a strange state of affairs, but possibly spoke to Khaled el Eloua's state of mind.

Another shot rang out. This time it took out the side window in the small shed directly in front of Jade.

Minutes ticked by, and the next shot told them that their sniper had somehow moved. The bullet kicked up dirt ten feet to his right. Whoever had them pinned was using the graveyard of implements as cover more efficiently than he could ever have imagined.

"Zafir," she hissed. With the shots now coming

from another angle, she'd had a chance to look into the shed, searching for a sign of their agent or Stanley's uncle. She moved away from the shed and back toward Zafir.

"I've found Anthony," she said, referring to their agent as she moved in beside him where he took cover behind the wheel of a tractor. "It's not good," she said. "He's not moving. I couldn't get inside, but I think he's dead."

Zafir spit out an expletive.

As he'd instructed earlier, Jade moved away, intent on covering the area from a different angle.

He had no time to consider the ramifications of what she'd found as he saw movement near the main house. He waited. A dark head. It was not Stanley's uncle. He fired once, twice, three times. Shots were answering his, and then it all stopped. A minute, two, he turned, checking for Jade. It was a mistake, something he wouldn't do with another agent. He couldn't help himself. He needed to know that she was okay.

A bullet whistled inches from him.

He nodded at Jade, now thirty feet away and just ahead of him, making her closer to the main house. He motioned with his right hand for her to move back, to shadow him, hopefully boxing in the man they suspected was Stan's cousin.

She fired before moving back. The bullet was low and did nothing but bite dirt.

Now the shots all seemed to be coming from a

small outbuilding that was close to the house. Another shot, but this time it went wild and was followed by seconds that turned into a minute of silence.

A shot from his left, Jade's position, and a thud ahead of him like their assailant had fallen. That was followed by silence.

Time seemed to spread out, seconds felt like minutes, and suddenly it appeared to be over. The gunman was down.

Jade stood up, took a step forward. There was movement ahead of him but it all happened so fast. And before he could warn her, even as he knew it was a mistake—it was too late.

"Get down!" he shouted. But everything was happening at lightning speed. The bullet spun her around and drove her to the ground. He crawled to her despite the danger.

"Blood," she whispered as her hand lifted from her chest.

His heart seemed to stop as he took her gun in his hand. Her weapon, his hand, everything was slick from her blood. With his gun in his right hand and her Colt in his left, he stood. It was a crazy thing to do but all he wanted was to begin shooting like a madman. To kill the son of a desert dog who had taken Jade down. Despite the insanity of what he did, he was lucky. For a split second he had a visual. That was all it took to take him out.

He heard his name or maybe he dreamed it,

dreamed that she was calling for him. Maybe he wished so badly to hear her voice once again that he had made fantasy a reality. He turned, crawling to her, but even as he assessed the damage, he saw the never-ending blood. And he knew that even a miracle might not be able to save her.

# Chapter Twenty-One

A Nassar employee had died in the line of duty, and another lay close to death. It was a sobering fact but the facts didn't get better.

Jade Van Everett was fighting for her life. Zafir didn't know what he would do if she died. He wasn't sure how it had happened, how he had failed to protect her or how he'd fallen in love with her.

With her down, he'd taken out Stanley's cousin, Fayad el Eloua, in a way he would never recommend to any of his agents. He had risen to his full height, thrown convention and reason away, and fired one shot after another until his magazine and Jade's was empty. In the end, the man had taken two fatal hits to the chest that had finally killed him.

It was over, but in a way it could never be over. The agent who had secured the estate had only recently been hired and trained. Anthony now lay in a morgue, and Jade's life hung in the balance. She was in intensive care with a bullet still lodged in her chest. It was touch and go whether she'd make it or not. The news ran through the agency with a sick kind of shock that only bad news can bring.

Zafir was tormented with remembering. In those horrible seconds after she'd been hit, he'd leaped out of character and shot again and again, without thought, without reason. He'd been driven by anger, rage and disbelief. He'd reacted instinctively, as no Nassar agent ever should.

Later, he'd refused to leave Jade's side. He'd used his own shirt to make a field dressing. Stanley's uncle had watched from a corner room in the mansion, ironically the one place his geriatric hearing couldn't hear the phone ring. It was there that he saw the man who threatened his life lose his. He had called for the emergency response team and immediately run out to help Zafir—talking constantly, a trick he said he'd learned in the army. He'd said that it was critical she remain conscious. Zafir hadn't remembered any of that at the time. They were memories that came back now in fits and starts as the long wait threatened his very soul, if not his sanity.

All of that had been the beginning of the nightmare. It felt like he'd been here, in this hospital, waiting—forever. A woman in a lab coat that drifted open and revealed lush curves walked by. He noticed because it was his job to notice, but for the first time, he had no interest. Jade was all that mattered. She had to live. He would die without her.

He didn't remember much of what happened in those first hours that stretched to days. It seemed like he was living in a movie that had been fast-forwarded, the actors switching and changing as the hours went on. And through it all, he stood with Jade's blood staining his shirt and the life of the woman he loved in someone else's hands. He knew now that if she died, there was no reason for him to live. He loved her that much; he loved her that wholeheartedly, that unselfishly. How or when this had happened, he didn't know. But when she took the bullet to the chest, he'd felt like the life had been ripped from him. He'd acted like a madman and fought back with all the firepower he had and with a deadly accuracy that had killed all that threatened them. He had taken out the one man who had done it, and then he'd taken her in his arms, trying to phone for help with one hand while trying to stop the bleeding with the other. He couldn't do it. He remembered the phone being taken from his hands. It was all a blur. In the hospital, he refused to leave her, and Talib had stuck around to make sure that he didn't kill himself in the process by forgetting to eat or sleep.

Even now he couldn't believe it. Somehow it felt like he had made this tragedy happen and as much as he knew that wasn't true, the thought wouldn't go away. He'd prided himself on keeping his agents safe. The fact that it had been Jade who orchestrated the assignment, the fact that every safeguard had been in place, none of it eased the responsibility that weighed heavily on him.

"You did everything you could," Emir said as he arrived an hour after Jade emerged from surgery. He patted him on the back.

"An agent is dead," he said grimly. He didn't say anything about Jade; he couldn't. For to admit that she was fighting for her life felt like it would make the worst happen.

"It's not your fault. Anthony was ordered to pull out, to wait for backup," Emir said. He shoved his hands in his pockets and met Zafir's look head-on. "You were in transit. There was nothing you could have done. It was Anthony who made the call, who reported Fayad's appearance. I don't know why he defied orders. But it definitely wasn't your fault. You had no say in any of it."

Zafir could feel his twin's pain. He knew that his heart ached at the outcome of his order. He almost wanted to say no, don't finish. But he knew that wasn't what needed to be done. Emir needed to say this.

"He was supposed to take Khaled, Stanley's uncle, and get out before any of this came down. But somehow something screwed up and he didn't go when he should." Emir shook his head. "This is on my shoulders."

"It's on no one's shoulders," Zafir said. "You made

the best decision you could. If you hadn't, more people might have died. There are so many other scenarios that could fall out, you know that. You can't predict the future. You can only do the best you can."

"I know," Emir agreed. "And I'll work through it."

After Emir left, Zafir was on his own again. He remembered what Emir had said. It didn't make what happened right, but as he told Emir, he could live with it, because the reality was there was no other choice, for either of them.

THE FIRST VOICE Jade heard, the first face she saw, the first hand she touched, was Zafir's. What she saw in his eyes, the connection that ran hot and electric between them, changed her in ways she'd never thought possible. Lust was one thing, but what she felt now was so much different. It was more powerful, more intangible than anything she'd felt for any other man. It went beyond lust or even love.

"Why are you here? Why aren't you on a case?" It was the first thing she could think to ask.

"Because I'd rather be with you," he replied.

She almost smiled. The spiritual connection that ran so deep only a few seconds ago was replaced with the familiar. His voice, molten tones of bass, his simple words of concern, seductive despite their surroundings. In fact, they brought a reality that took her away from her surroundings, from the doctors, the nurses, the needles and the pain.

They didn't talk much that day or the next. The pain and discomfort were too great. But a week after she was fully conscious and sitting up, they talked.

"How long have I been here?"

"Weeks," he said loosely.

"And you've been here all that time?"

"Where else would I be?"

She blinked and seemed not to focus on him. It was as if she were seeing something or someone else.

"It was you?" she said. "Every time I woke up. I could sense you."

"You knew I was here," he said softly.

"I needed you here," she replied.

She closed her eyes and slept.

## Chapter Twenty-Two

The last weeks had been tough. But Jade was finally well on the road to recovery. In fact, only two days ago she'd been discharged and by the end of the week she'd be clear to fly. But they were taking it easy, and at the end of the week Zafir took her on a shorter flight. They made the trip out to the estate near Rabat where Stanley was now living. The case they had been assigned to protect Stanley had been closed with the shoot-out that had almost killed Jade. There was no one alive who was a threat to Stanley or his uncle any longer. Now it was time to say goodbye.

Stanley sat on the sprawling front veranda of the mansion of his uncle's estate.

"This is goodbye, Stan," he said as he approached. It had been three weeks since they'd first stepped foot in Morocco, intent on closing this case. "How's your Uncle Khaled?"

"Doing great. I'm glad I'm here for him. That he survived my cousin's greed." He smiled.

"And you survived to keep his legacy alive."

"I did. Thanks to you and Jade. Odd, my relatives, except for him—" he glanced over his shoulder where his uncle was walking toward one of the outbuildings, a dog following slowly behind him "—are so twisted. My brother, two cousins." He shook his head. "Makes you think it could be genetic."

"You turned out fine, Stan," Zafir assured him. "Anyway, it's over, and we just wanted to come and say goodbye and let you know that next time you visit Wyoming it won't be quite as hair-raising as your last visit."

"Is that an invitation?"

"It is," Zafir said with a smile.

"I may take you up on that. Maybe even next year, but if I do, I'll look you up." He shook his head. "In fact, I'll hire you."

Zafir laughed. "The danger's past, Stan."

"I don't know about that," he replied with a smile. "My crazed cousins might be gone, but there's still a rancher or two that I wouldn't turn my back on."

Zafir smiled. He held out his hand. "Deal. Till next summer."

He turned, looking to where Jade was chatting with Stanley's uncle. The old man laughed and clapped a hand on her shoulder.

"She's something, isn't she?" Stanley asked the question not like a man who had any romantic interest in a woman but more with a hint of admiration. "If I had a sister, I'd want her to be just like her."

"She definitely had your back this whole time," Zafir said. "Nassar is lucky to have her."

"You're lucky to have her," Stanley said. "Don't think I haven't seen what's going on between you two." He smiled.

"What's going on?" Jade asked as she came up to the two men.

"Nothing," Zafir said, feeling heat crawl up his neck as if he'd been caught doing something he shouldn't have been. He hadn't had that feeling in a very long time. "Stan was just saying how great you are at your job."

"I'm going to miss you, Stanley," Jade said. "You definitely keep things exciting."

"What, by offering near-death experiences?"

Jade laughed. "I love the new Stanley."

"Stan," he said. "I prefer Stan." He stood up from where he was sitting on the steps. "Thanks, both of you."

He reached out and shook Zafir's hand. "Do you mind?" he asked.

"I don't care what he says, I'm not leaving without a hug, Stan," she said with a smile.

"I never thought it would end like this," Stan said a minute later. He wiped the back of his hand across his cheek as a large shaggy black dog shoved his head against his thigh, and a small brown mixed breed barked shrilly. "I'm back, boys. It's over."

THEY FLEW HOME later the next week. Jade was up and swearing she was fully recovered. But despite her protests, Zafir insisted on carrying her suitcase.

Now they were halfway home.

"I imagine this may be the easiest assignment we see in a long time," Jade said with a soft purr as she ran a finger down Zafir's chest. "At least it started out easy."

"I don't know about easiest. Maybe the most deceptive might be a better description," he said with a laugh. "Did I tell you I was elated when the case was upgraded and terrified for you at the same time?"

"Elated?"

"Chance to work with you, my love," he said with a contented growl as he pulled her into his arms.

The case had been one of the most challenging, but only because the growing attraction between them had been a distraction. His hands ran the length of her. His fingers were gentle as they moved down the silken skin over the sweet curves that had him hot and hard without the suggestion of anything but her nakedness beneath him. They had won this case together. And in the weeks that she had fought for her life, he had realized what she meant to him, and more importantly, what it would mean to lose her.

"You've got to quit doing that," she said.

"What?"

"Worrying, and worse, protecting me. We won't be able to work together otherwise."

"I'm not sure if I can do that, but maybe I can camouflage my feelings."

She laughed, the sound a light tinkle that stirred something deep in his heart.

"You're going to have to do better than that."

"I'll try," he said, and was surprised that he meant it. He knew how much Nassar meant to her, as it did to him. It was just that she meant so much more.

Now she leaned against the jet's butter-soft leather recliner seat and sighed at the feel of Zafir's fingers massaging her feet.

"Heaven," she murmured.

"Ah, my dear. Not quite, but one day I'll show you heaven, at least here on earth." He let go of her foot and stood up, leaning over to offer her a gentle kiss that only hinted at passion.

"Is it always going to be like this between us?" Her words were a throaty whisper, her breath hot and seductive against his neck.

His lips again met hers, this time claiming them as his own with a passion that he'd held back in that first kiss.

"I can't see it any other way," he said thickly as he lifted up on one knee and his caresses drifted to other places.

Her phone whistled, the sound signaling a new

case. And despite his protests only a day ago, she'd taken her physician's last advice before she left Morocco and declared herself ready to work.

His phone whistled in unison.

"Timing," he muttered as his hand lingered on her breast, feeling the hardening of her nipple that offered so much more.

"Is always off," she finished.

Below them, as the company jet streaked across the remaining miles, the crystal blue of a Wyoming spring sky was alight with a promise that paled against the feel of her skin beneath his fingers.

And as she rose up to meet him, they both knew that no matter where this new case might take them, home was here, in each other's arms.

\* \* \* \* \*

*Ryshia Kennie's miniseries*
DESERT JUSTICE
*continues next month with*
*SON OF THE SHEIK.*

*You'll find it wherever*
*Harlequin Intrigue books are sold!*

## COMING NEXT MONTH FROM
## ◧ HARLEQUIN®

# INTRIGUE

### Available May 23, 2017

### #1713 HOT ZONE
*Ballistic Cowboys* • by Elle James
Army ranger Trace "Hawkeye" Walsh has no choice but to assist tough-as-nails rancher Olivia Dawson after he incapacitates her foreman, but his involvement on the ranch uncovers a dark conspiracy...and their own desires.

### #1714 CAVANAUGH STANDOFF
*Cavanaugh Justice* • by Marie Ferrarella
With a serial killer sweeping through Aurora, Detective Ronan Cavanaugh O'Bannon will do whatever it takes to protect one of Cavanaugh's own—even swallow his pride and work with wild-card detective Sierra Carlyle.

### #1715 THE WARRIOR'S WAY
*Apache Protectors: Tribal Thunder* • by Jenna Kernan
The entire city of Phoenix is under threat by ecoterrorists, and Turquoise Guardian and tribal police chief Jack Bear Den is working closely with loose cannon former FBI operative Sophie Rivas to save the day, even if it brings their dangerous attraction to the surface...

### #1716 MURDER IN BLACK CANYON
*The Ranger Brigade: Family Secrets* • by Cindi Myers
An FBI agent is murdered. A US senator goes missing. Loner PI Kayla Larimer will need to learn to trust Lieutenant Dylan Holt if she's going to make the connection between these crimes and the mysterious cult camped in the hostile Colorado wilderness.

### #1717 BODYGUARD WITH A BADGE
*The Lawmen: Bullets and Brawn* • by Elizabeth Heiter
Juliette Lawson is desperate to stay hidden from her dangerous cop ex-husband—desperate enough to take FBI sniper Andre Diaz hostage in order to escape Quantico—but when Andre learns the truth of her past, he knows he's the man to keep her safe.

### #1718 SON OF THE SHEIK
*Desert Justice* • by Ryshia Kennie
After a one-night stand with playboy and investigator Talib Al-Nassar left her pregnant, Sara Elliott fled Morocco, but when she returns to teach her son about his roots her secret is discovered—and the only man with the power to protect her son is his father.

# I N T R I G U E

*Detective Ronan Cavanaugh O'Bannon will do
whatever it takes to protect one of the Cavanaughs' own
from a serial killer sweeping through Aurora, including
working with wild-card detective Sierra Carlyle.*

*Read on for a sneak preview of*
*CAVANAUGH STANDOFF,*
*the next book in* USA TODAY *bestselling author*
**Marie Ferrarella***'s fan-favorite series*
*CAVANAUGH JUSTICE.*

He knew he had to utilize her somehow, and maybe
she could be useful. "All right, you might as well come
along. You might come in handy if there's a next of kin
to notify." Ronan began walking back to his car. "I'm not
much good at that."

"I'm surprised," Sierra commented.

Reaching the car, Ronan turned to look at her. "If
you're going to be sarcastic—"

"No, I'm serious," she told him, then went on to
explain her rationale. "You're so detached, I just assumed
it wouldn't bother you to tell a person that someone
they'd expected to come home was never going to do that
again. It would bother them, of course," she couldn't help
adding, "but not you."

Ronan got into his vehicle, buckled up and pulled
out in what seemed like one fluid motion, all the while

chewing on what this latest addition to his team had just said. Part of him just wanted to let it go. But he couldn't.

"I'm not heartless," he informed her. "I just don't allow emotions to get in the way and I don't believe in using more words than are absolutely necessary," he added pointedly since he knew that seemed to bother her.

"Well, lucky for you, I do," she told him with what amounted to the beginnings of a smile. "I guess that's what'll make us such good partners."

He looked at her, stunned. He viewed them as being like oil and water—never able to mix. "Is that your take on this?" he asked incredulously.

"Yes," she answered cheerfully.

The fact that she appeared to have what one of his brothers would label a "killer smile" notwithstanding, Ronan just shook his head. "Unbelievable."

"Oh, you'll get to believe it soon enough," she told him. Before he could say anything, Sierra just continued talking to him and got down to the immediate business at hand. "I'm going to need to see your files on the other murders once we're back in the squad room so I can be brought up to date."

He didn't even spare her a look. "Fine."

"Are you always this cheerful?" she asked. "Or is there something in particular that's bothering you?"

*Don't miss*
*CAVANAUGH STANDOFF by Marie Ferrarella,*
*available June 2017 wherever*
*Harlequin® Intrigue books and ebooks are sold.*

www.Harlequin.com

# THE WORLD IS BETTER WITH

## Romance

Harlequin has everything from contemporary, passionate and heartwarming to suspenseful and inspirational stories.

Whatever your mood,
we have a romance just for you!